TODAY YESTERDAY
AFTER MY DEATH

ISBN: 978-1-916541-05-4

First edition.

First published in 2024 by Erratum Press
Sheffield, UK
www.erratumpress.com

Design and typesetting by Ansgar Allen
Cover detail from the Bourbaki Panorama
Illustration of a solar analemma by the author

Segments of this novel have appeared (in various forms):
A Minor, ANNEXE, *Arts Society of Kingston Poetic
License, The Ekphrastic Review, Entropy Magazine, Lincoln
Review, Hyades Magazine, Journal of Compressed Arts,
Periodicity, Poetry Distillery, Telephone: A Game of Art
Whispered Around the World, Tnsfet*, & *Verse Ville*. In the
anthologies: *Montreal Poetry Prize Anthology 2022*; *Beyond
the Frame* (Diode Editions); and at Longleaf Press. In
chapbooks: *Sweetwater Ardour* (Yavinkika Press), *Come,
Ghost* (Triple Series, Ravenna Press/forthcoming). In the
poetry collection *Arbor Vitae* (Nauset Press) and *Tender to
Empress* (Visual Poetics with Wet Cement Press). In film by
Anthony M Sannazzaro (through Plants Painting Poetry).

TODAY YESTERDAY AFTER MY DEATH

Maureen Alsop

ERRATUM PRESS

To trace a solar analemma, the observer maintains a singular position as the sun's declination cycles an infinite path…

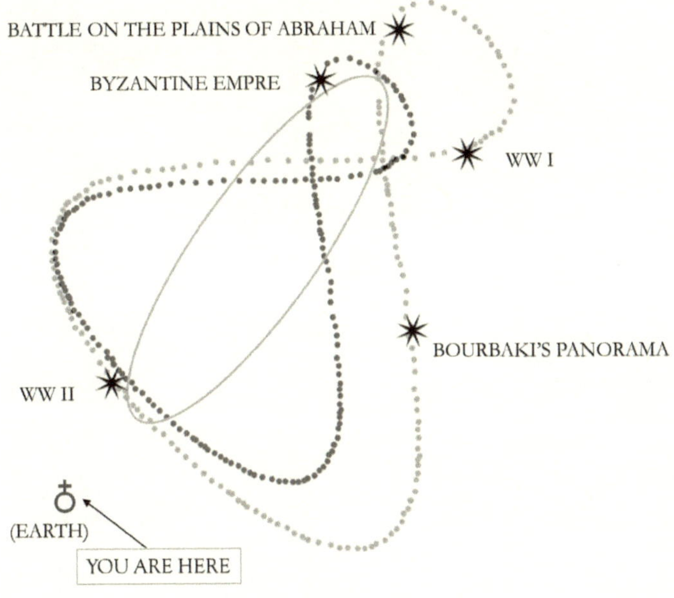

WHO WE WERE

You = Consciousness, the transferable understanding, one who observes, listens, transposes, the reader, the writer, (technically you, I, he, she, all)
Death = Personification, the universal inescapable, the first person "I"
The Dead = Visitants, Revenants, those traveling the roads of the afterlife
Magdalene/She = She rests on and off the edges— a ghost who doesn't realize she has died
Unnamed Soldier = He appears in Magdalene's thoughts and disappeared in battle
Unnamed Narrator = like all other characters here listed, a universal ghost, a presence observing the epochs

$$\nabla$$

Is this the pasture where I died or am I underwater?

I would rather your headstone, a blue insomnia, be a point where strings tug the surface of uncertainty.

How might I describe you as I remember.

O remember.

4

We did not die in our dying, she said.

You never understood you were already dead.

I died continuously.

I saw you, and once thought you were real.

I'll come back. I'll come in numerous apparitions. And walk into the room, soundless.

I have said it many nights, just as you are, I am alive among The Dead.

There were so many versions of a single battle. I didn't know where to begin.

The newly dead are brought to me loosely in catalogues, driftwood cairns, and hessian boots rotted in snow. I, like they, were beyond most anything now. The Dead bring disembodied language, transmissions, and are gone into gesture. You don't have to remember the archaic phrases, the madness which shows itself through their strange tellings. You don't have to remember me. You don't have to withhold the praise of trees that love the sun. There is no easy way toward.

I will not close my heart to their signallings. It is the transmission which connects me phrase by phrase to grandmothers and fathers so far past we can barely hear. I am breaching the cold descent of ice caps. The language of death is an old skin.

How many centuries deepened. You, a ghost, lay unearthed. You knew the settlers. They were calm. They steadied themselves against boulder, against arrow. Now they abide among leaves spread through the moraines. Not looking into the mouths of The Dead was my triumph. A neutral measure against mass graves, as exposure leads to complacency.

And you want to be alive. So, it's to you that I'm held, talking. Think of this as an entopic graphomania, a process where the artist laces ink pinpricks across an old book, a newspaper, a blank sheet of paper, and then draws lines all about the page making a pattern or a bit of a mess depending on how you interpret the result. Let that be us. Let us be that joy.

Yes, she fed the horses, but was it *"I"* in the story. Was it *"you"* in the story. I don't remember.

I am death myself falling over the leaves the waters the particles of every silence.

In the trenches with your ghost, I became. I became ghost among men.

I lived with you mostly, there, amid disjointed incidents.

I never wanted to be a lesser hero. As a stranger, I came among you. Prepared for the place you were headed. Truth is only alive when there is witness. The true thing is found only in the body. It surely waits to move.

At night we heard killing sounds catch along the road's shallow chalk lines. My horse, a good horse, walked backwards. Backward, over the graves of the living, we walked into the second battle where I found you.

I am the ghost you asked to stay. I am meant to assuage your guilt, but I said no.

I am a person of no importance.

It is hard now to read people's circumstance. I've lost motivation for how I am to see life.

We were the punished and would never answer to the land.

I remember his face as he moved quickly past. I remember you, my enemy.

That night I followed the scarred trail where the horse stripped the timothy and quack grass. I found square lettering in the clearing where fingers once turned pages. I stood and watched as if leaning against a fourth doorway. Pausing, I heard carriages carried away, a series of trees thudding under a locking axe. I held a need to name the horses. A warmth greased their bodies and glass walls enclosed the pasture. The pasture fills with smoke. I disappeared into a photograph of fire. It was in my sleep you returned.

Δ

TODAY YESTERDAY
AFTER MY DEATH

During the pre-war, the peasants slept in the stable, died of starvation or were dragged out by cowards and shot near the chapel. The outer gate near the cemetery, where the killings took place, blushed in moss. In later years the entry paled into in a patch of mica. In my mind I sit in this pallid circle and gather each revolutionary's corpse. I lift their chest to my chest. My mouth emits a light upon their lips, as a blue frost rises to filter their breath through my windpipe.

Δ

BYZANTINE EMPIRE

‡

Trial By Ordeal

I don't know how she did it.

But from time to time, I remember, said The Dead.

They had her—and her slightness in death.

It was like August in December, and her earliest betrayal washed through the grassland. The bird's dispersals gathered the trees.

A woman, the opposite in her attributes to this moss which grows against the skin, limitless and without longing.

These years mirror the woods which float in her eyes. A witch's bargain with the heavens. They found a sachet of cloves in her pocket. There is a trace of a door—beyond the opposite of her death—into which she is drawn. Even this full of winter, the currents continued to expand. Given the pleats in the water, I might explain time's levelled effect.

Only you are left in the discourse, as if her beliefs were suicide.

A soldier met her at the quick curves of the river. All the sumac lowering into her chest, a summer snowbed, her shoulders lost among bracken.

We came, said The Dead.

All the unnatural visitors came.

Looking through blades of grass, not looking with their eyes, as she crossed the plains.

You said, *I know you.*

*

Is there a need yet to explain a split in our consciousness?

Where the moss grows, where the moss grows, someone places a blanket over the earth, a blue fur, a luminous flora. The sky expands a dark wash as fire burns over the waters. Fire on the tip of the tongue. Fire on the iron roof, fire surrounding the ventricle within the house, the last chamber and the first. She would burn and she would rest. She would rest she would rest she would rest and after. After the war she would no longer touch you like a stranger.

When she reviews the setting in her mind she imbues the ruins with restraint, the summer mosaics were always a fragment of injunctions. She stares at the ceiling. A calm triangular light spills from the window. The weathered bodies float on her desk. They are small anatomies of fingerprint, self-portraits in blind contour, effigies of chiselled balsa, a graveyard room.

Survival is named by the imagination. She believes the tension of love is bound by space, gravity an example of violence. Wonder is imbalance. They followed a trail of flies to her house.

Bees navigate through an echo chamber. They rise in the manger, the armoury, the mezzanine—these places whereupon the simple shift in the helix elicits a slurry of telegrams. She was a woman, awkward without exception, who waited.

She spent years composing letters, a glazed serif, the ink splattered gothic, hour under hour her quill tip tore the paper's edge.

Intimately thin lines emerged under terror's clockwork. The external references to dark were made whole. She disappeared into the threat of pain while the ones who faced death stopped corresponding. She's forgotten the phrases, the confinements, the ease with which she foresaw their hangings, the construction sites, the notices.

They'd been sloppy with their bayonets, their machetes, but clean under the commands. The armies retained a place within the realms of the holy. They never saw the damage.

Wind and dust flattened the harvest and brought famine.

The legend arose with her arrival, the ice-covered carriage held her casket. Snow's civilization cleared the northeast canal. In the village cemetery, where customary wreaths arranged headstones, Magdalene monitored the wind. Repetition of cloud evoked dialect. The sound confirmed a question.

From where did her shame depart.

The last time you saw her, her haloed shoulder slouched into the splintered side of the barn beneath sleep's taxidermy dark.

She would be chastened by patterns at the crossroad. She would give up the afterlife. She would pull the famine out of the garden with orchards on fire.

You fingered Saint Michael's textbook, the pages laid the angels in resin, their wings opened like baptismal birds. A ritual of finches, a musical species, expanded the basin of holy water as they separated the fresco. An ibis read the oiled pages. They dipped their beaks, failed arrows of ornamental descent. Hazel trees and lilies quavered in the knoll.

All the men in town were gone when you returned. Orchards, rancid in pollen's decay, chastened a slow surrender, and saying the unsaid, in what she wouldn't want to say, says: *It is said now. We loved who we loved.*

She could only be what we obsessed of her. The men still think she's the devil, even after all the evidence.

‡

Where The Dead live everything is confession, and at the prison where she found them, there were no borders, no walls. The enemy threatened to kill her. But the threat of death does not deter someone who has been beaten all over her body. In her head she convinced herself there was no other option. She'd been like this so long. Arbitrary threats and arrests, endless interrogations. She wrote of the second death in the province. It was on the anniversary of the first death. She'd taken note of it in nearly every page of the ledger. Each notation a symbol, like something scratched into the walls of a cave. Perpendicular stones break into sand. The wind never eases. They took Magdalene at the risk of spreading disease to the other prisoners, and the other prisoners watched her being pulled by her hair and tossed into a cell with overflowing sewage. Her view to hang herself wasn't working so she stopped. The weight stripped off her; all along she knew justice wouldn't arrive. She was a single pixel in the entire field of view. Her succour, her sorrow. The incident occurred, but not where you thought nor how. For centuries the valley held the bones of the enemy. The horses and men remained scattered and abandoned long after the retreat. A revolutionary trail of exile disappeared through peaceful periods and re-emerged without explanation. They were looking for admittance. She came at ease within herself. There was a gift she loved. They never came to an understanding. She didn't know where this was going. The old grief or the new. The love in her voice was the sound of holiness and sorrow. A voice that walks and starts and remains fit for remonstration, for domesticity. As if there is a light-switch in the corridor to flick that will shift the mind. It was always the same fire. The same river. The same mass burial. There was no moon. In the dark hush there were times of shame. Times of waiting. As if coming to an end not forced, but soon, too soon, a lateral violence, the voice of the man who died. The voice that told The Dead to take shelter in the grass where the grass is wide and tall. On the last day, the door was open, but she wouldn't walk through it. She'd been seeking the answer a long time. The air, wide with grief, and her grief itself, wide. They threw their weapons to the ground. She threw her weapon. She threw her body into the outer air in liberation as if throwing herself into the ocean.

‡

The constellation: an arrow, a serpent, she read the foreleg and jawbone, she spat as the stars shifted east of your right shoulder. All the planets misaligned. She fingered her own forehead, a triangle impressed upon the curve of her brow. She could see them. *Forgive me—* The Dead say.

At the Saintes-Maries-de-la-Mer wetlands the sky stirs. She continued to mark the azimuth— sacrosanct and without discipline, without foreknowledge, without instinct. Her automaticity as desire, the sun squaring upon the Camargue delta— as the delta itself engulfs the earth. Time as topography. A recurrent death, a recurrent disappointment, a series of erratic, incurious waves. Transcendence, time's equation, remains unaffected by death.

As you knew it: the strange banks of Magdalene's stone house, silent shores, downs and dark, the sea's night-window murmured. Tides glittering like tiny claws, your logic settled with her as you settled some compass, some internal ship un-shored.

You wade through crescent pools wound through two ruts along the channel, deeper as you settle at the bottom of the sea. You perch upon ancient stones, fire's thousand shields around you. Held in abeyance, you said you'd had enough. Had held out enough. You spoke of winners and losers. You grieved for her. You grieved for her. She did not grieve for you.

You wanted to go back, to tell her, and when you say "you", you may mean "I" or "she" or "him" or "us." You wanted to tell her to stay put under the tributary's spell, the cottonwood's sway, to remember the elder's provisions, but consciousness, in truth, is not resolved along a singular directive.

Magdalene culled notes from the ledgers and old notebooks, receipts, and to-do lists. Years and years of jottings. These were movements toward her end stage. Horizons and illusions. *The transgressions before me were many—* said Death. Her ledger recounts:

∴

Sometimes I wake. I wake up and feel I am a ghost no one sees…

Though gone, I interweave the code of my body's static through time's action with space, not to demarcate a series of events, but to devise the cellular impact of a new lexicon. Think of it like a barnacle, a growth expanding off my old voice, one that you still recognize, layered beneath this new one. I am attached still. Here to give you instinct.

I don't think you meant for it to happen, and in the beginning, you didn't know what summoned them over the hills as the mob and the city's ruins crept toward the room of my death. There was no order to the experience.

And I too, as if with eyes sewn shut… I sought my husband…

The ambient environment changes when we are physically in love.

The original goal was your perspective, and from your perspective, the goal: to understand human memory, how it holds violence, the way it transcends grief. The template of human nature: riddled with sharp edges.

Miles of sandstorms and what seemed like meteors … the cottage battered… floods all through the garrison town where the elders were hung. Speak to me on the physics of grief. Why…still among the inhuman confusion… did I find hope…

∴

Before she died, before you died, Magdalene was wandering the road and stood in a little thicket at the foot of a tree. You met her at a clearing on the lane to High Wood. At a crossroad, now a modern boundary, an old Romen lime, she stood before you, luminous between the earth burnt sky and her earth burnt skin. Her vermillion robe hid the indigo shadows of her loose hair. You held reverence, but you concede, you misread people badly. You heard she bred doves, worshipped a human skull, and carried a scarlet egg in a basket. You heard at night she lay on a hairshirt between the rocks.

She didn't know her other ghost, the disembodied horizon you and The Dead walked, nor of her death in this battle or others. You held her courage as the wind beat you. She retreated from the voices of The Dead, an infusion from the past or future, she heard their breath, particles caught in her throat, the last battle of the First Crusade, a few molecules surfacing centuries later mingled with the firebombs, the future's kill space. Her voice was the sound between the sound of the artillery tanks and the rustle of spear grass. A half singing began above the charred copse. A voice beyond her voice, a heretic's tongue, a rasp, a sound as blood: burnt, thick and deep among the trees, the understory, the tectonic shift breaking the horizons into an upward scale. The dawn turned slowly its zenith toward you, a pale ash drawn dawn through her gaze. She remembered the house where she was born, a place in a dream. A dream she was transient in dreaming, tugging at the wind, the glass door, and the night expanding.

You bade each other in. You were her dream repeating, and she was a dream you entered. She kept a ledger and tracked the evolution of you as a consciousness. Perhaps you were a river moving past or a pattern on a leaf. You were structures, you were both surprises to one another.

The revolution you were a part of became your identity, and within days, a language, the charge of a passionate new belief. You heard god stabbing pinholes into the heavens, uncharted records, points of decay marked progress. Fallow stars hallowed sunlit dunes. Slight signallings you were alive. Your pockets filled with dust as the landscape crumbled. It seemed you were born with the essence of a beast. The always sky, the always water, the brink of reassurance as your destruction. Equuleus above, scent of camphor among the clamour. You see things which shape faith as you go on moving—a strange nostalgia: restless, unnamed. Your thoughts are draft horses making figure eights; you go round and round the damage, the repetitions of grief stalled and stung Magdalene's dreams. Every war requires the sound of a plural diction. A language beneath and above the earth, the conduit of language, a soldier, an echo, the living ghost before destruction. Obliteration holds a fresh articulation, constraint elided. Who keeps you alive. The eighth consciousness repeats. The sun unfolds. The soul's end exists as a source of dispute.

She gave you her mind without hesitation. Her thoughts echoed a great freedom, pain, and contemplation. She spoke often of The Dead—this one, you, who stood before her, and those ghosts unknown who crowded around you. There were lost sounds and many papers she loved: sheets inked in thick, unintelligible scrawls. The insistence of her voice met death's immortality. There was nothing to do; nothing to do but to follow her trail, a loop of ascensions and declinations, a solar analemma's snare. In her presence, the cinder and the aftermath, illusion lit upon a silvering lemniscate. An equation spread above as an antidote. You were both grounded to one spot: an agonic line stretched between the hemispheres, shifting with her breath. The sun was ending. The sun surrendered. The sun, in its risen point, circular in certain beliefs, dives in steady signals. It's a surface dusk, the whole of mid-noon maps each night's silence. It vanishes over a bridge year by year as ultramarine birds darken the pasture. Constellations disappeared into the gloss of her calculations. With thanks, grace passed between you, and you were ready to send light to the moment death's victory set in.

You listen only when The Dead have doubt. You listen with self-denial as their denial. A pocketsize metamorphosis, their last words, and Magdalene's ledger to carry. A ledger into which she impresses the balance of action from one battle through the next. She was to listen to the dying in ease and ascension. Recording only the transgressions of the sun above which corresponded to the belief in beauty, momentary terrains, pivot points. The sun above, the cosmology, she identified as both aversion and rapture, with no more sense of location, other than where you began. The Dead were not abandoned. She did not abandon them, but an emptiness adhered like the wrappings of a pharaoh; bit by bit the bodily phases faded absolutely.

A tremor of dust lifts off the plan and braises Magdalene's face. You sat down beside her. In her eyes you saw the weight of The Dead.

You wanted to attend to a certain penitence. One which you could understand.

Magdalene is a conscious soul with which you are entangled.

‡

When I was young, I was in an accident and someone died, Magdalene said.

You could see traces, rock-strewn visions, her wild survival, etched nightly in her eyes, rapid dilations shifting among the forces of her sleep. Backlit, a refraction, a leaning-in to all that came alive. In a collection of points, she diagrammed the missing as she looked up into the constellations. Above her sternum she positioned a double dagger of her own making, the last broken sword, the Lorraine cross. Her eyes gleamed against the slick grass of the sky. Both open earth and iris blinked in a frozen varnish. Her complexion, water's torrent at the edge of a far creek bed, flushed as she slipped back into the trees. You could see snow-mounds sheltering an ice-frozen house. It was so close to her skin's surface as if looking sharp down the barrel of a shotgun.

The road was bare when you walked back into the night, but it was difficult, as if marching through brush. The dead voices fused under the bewildered weight she carried in her throat as she tracked her reflection over the floodplain's blue mirror. She caught the tide's trance, a traffic she claimed among the rusted military waters and ibis' footprints. Her voice, in totemic patterns, led them through ravines of wet grass. Love's hunger dissipated desire. No longer masked, a triple signal between ghosts rose from her lowest joy as a tremor between the plashes of The Dead, and amber grains of dust thrust up through her lungs. She spoke to The Dead, as if she spoke from within them. They knew she may be the one. The envoy to annihilate the last of them. When they reached the base that morning, The Partisans summoned them one by one.

‡

When the sun fades, you stand still beside a bonfire into which you'll go cold and missing at the centre. The pyre marks your first hunger. This warmth is a confused expression. Trial by fire, the comfortless nothing, a remnant jawbone defies the coal. You fingered the symbols. Not the deep dagger, the infinite, the pilcrow, not the addax, nor owl, nor broad axe, not the Lorraine cross, not the triangular ideogram of god, nor the Camargue cross, and not yet even the ampoule hanging from a ribbon at Magdalene's waist. The marking of stars, time's constellations began with loss. You smeared ash, the taste of blood on the dirt.

She was an embodiment of a space between worlds, an edge where the unconsciousness of the earth is pure. She never touched the ground. She progressed through one point in time while observing another. A synaptic response, her light leveling the fault lines. Half-burned, half-buried in the sun-crusted sky, in fragment, she was like the clean earth. Embodied, exposed and strange. At the shattered mile at Verdun, she travelled through a crater shaped like a wing. It radiated white like Roman marble in the mud. She went early through the dark and found the stone. She travelled down as if from a ferryman's light, a light which opens to cross death's channel, a light darkness follows. As if her wounds were natural.

Light soon registers the forest trees. It is the instinct of matter to belong, a finality of desire, despite the "few" or the "one" lost. Love eases love. When it comes, comes the tide. It is like every breaking. She stands by the stone and weeps; turns her back and then lays beside you into her weeping. It is the half naming of silence. It is basic. It is the depths of the steep waters where the coral drops off. It's the cairn that the masses gathered from the pit where you lay buried. She shook with the infirmities of angels.

The sun was a seam in which you might place yourselves. Magdalene stared into the creatures of dust, galactic beetles as an ignorant dirt of an endless soot. Within the limits there are gross achievements and a sense of efficacy. Birds in tawny waves thickened the window out of which you sought the night-horizon. Vaseline glass, oil cloth, your perceptions glazed by human hurts, the delusion of your terms here— recurrent and difficult.

Will I die if I talk with you these minutes... she whispers. Magdalene went early through the dark and found your headstone. A stone the size of her palm sealed a cave's entrance.

You start. You are filled in silence. Death quietly reaches one way. *One way I fought the other*—you said— *I knew you would tell me to pick one. A she, or a her, an I or a you. But consciousness is multi-fold. I refuse.* She heard his disembodied anger through the rubble. He didn't know who he was, he didn't remember he was you. O reader, you, be atoned to the crossing...

Magdalene's ledger records a trespass through the crusades at Civetot:

∴

> *When I went into battle with you, the field opened without incident. Without incident, I lost my mind. I lost my mind.*

And on the battlefield, I lost my leg. Not necessarily in that order. What failed me. A premonition drawn between us. A person really. But he wasn't the enemy. He was on our conscience. The quarter century's slow surrender. The late arrivals trembled. The soldiers prepared to fight.

I knew his profile, knew the back of his neck when he bowed, the phrases made speechless, my throat, as I pushed against language, pushed against a late desire. I held my shoulders to the fire. To make myself love, I forgot what I didn't want. My skin cut open. His eyes, a formula of admission, almost cold, almost aggrieved. There was a way of alighting the other, a way to remember what was ignored.

No, I didn't want that sort of love.

∴

‡

Many times, you lay in the old battlefields, unconscious, and found yourself as if walking through a passage. A black dust over the grey valley, the sound of women weeping. Just as the treaty papers lay, in their peculiar speak, splintered arrows pierce your tongue, you draw your signature in two directions across the plain.

The crypt lay open in her mind, along the edge of the field where her body washed up. She could hear his breath like an oath.

AN UNNAMED SOLDIER'S BURIAL CAVE: OATH AFTER THE BATTLE OF CIVETOT

His lungs were lifting and awake, and he held the whole darkness of the stone wall in his breath, and he held his ribs in his hands. And he resented life. And he resented this wish for life. He resented this hour he awoke. His legs stirred and he moved. Bandages from his face and from his knees, where he had been struck, fell away.

He lay among the petrichor, the dry lichen, desireless, watching the last cost: the cold settling around him. Dark, snowy light pressing through the cracks of the cave. A strange amber coloured marigold, a waxen lantern—the sun, rigid and transparent, braised his forehead. The sun, a lacerated blossom, rose, scented by frost.

A doe is shedding a dream of birch, goldenrod, ragweed. Shedding a mouthful of lullabies and bracken. Her clumsy heartbeat, a procession, his hush in her ear. He hears the sun breaking him. In ardour, in sweetwater. His family was waiting. Dusk above them, the scent of dark, a foam bathing his hands as if in a mirror, the face of the anointed. Their faces in reflection. *I don't understand. How does it end. Tell me: how does it end.* He slow sheds the chart of his oppositions, his symbols—his body falling into charts, in certain empathy, as certain obstacle. Whatever tenderness awakens the will, won't awaken. Vowels blow across their limbs as he is calling closer. Autumn stirs in the vetiver. His wishes spill into the wind and grasses upward along the length of the embankment; it is their breath when he was singing. His breath, a great revenge, a great sorrow. The doe yields. It is the last syllable of her breath. It is a great sleep. A sleep in which he realized there'd never been a location. Fire tears through the grass, a midpoint turn, the doe looking back, kicking.

Yes, a slowness, his family waiting, across the plateau, a tremble of dust folding into the violet understory. Froth washing across the ankle-deep sea. The old words came, necessary in bereavement. The first twilight, the green moon; the sound of paper folded under the slowness, under the splayed sun. They bring cosmology, they bring love. They carry the sweet succour of old rain. Ancestors, in great sorrow, a salted spark he cannot see, but their image, a coursing, opal red that impales the veins of his eyelids with old images, bison, aurochs, lions floating in tributaries along gypsum cracks.

I cannot speak.

His memory was in place, and he was hurt by the memory.

A premonition of the body was the memory of death.

Through the copper scented night, through traces in the scent of blood, they'd come. He could read them. A life in the mind of The Dead reaches the living. Like the serpent's milk, the zephyr, and the owl.

He'd moved through the battle. It was hard and he would fight again. Death is the last battle from which he'd risen. *Death, a hard battle I've lost and lost. And I would fight again.*

The silence, a thick silence, wakes blinding through the waters of his death, immutable and transparent. A gold wave passes above the cobalt hills. Dim sunlight unifies autumn, an azoic autumn's mica sun. Quietly, footstep traces and frozen stones, scored by ice, dissolve. Nothing moves. Those relatives alone in the wind, vibrant in the dark spears, as if spread and slanting between the trees, detached among the fractions and rays, there is something adverse, something that advances through the granite corridors. Consciousness surges. It is a gathering wasteland; stone fruits and hoar apples fall through the branches of the trees; the limitations are a dizzying hunger. A siege, voices weaving in a shrill dominion, grew thick about him.

Traces of winter were here along the damp earth, along the edges of the limestone, the tomb itself now his body, a surface altering between mud and air, his thigh bone between stone walls, the stone, a cold atonement hidden in the granite inlet.

His mother's face soaked in violet shades of death. Her death, an immensity. An echo past the cavern, something rose far and inaudible, a voice radiated as if from under him, as if from within. Hearing too, a shift in the grass, a gallop, a mare, or the sea blanking, murmuring, and calling; a constant desire, a repentance above the tree leaves where the sky entraps the mountains. A great sea flooded over him. Magdalene sipped at the sky, and she swallowed and she drank her death. *I am no one. I am dust. I am called toward you. I am lain among the lost ones.* There was a way to read the earth as desire— like dawn, a thin recognition, numb, resolute, hungered, and battered. He and The Dead were brought closer into her vision.

He was only there in one dimension. The only dimension you may travel into the right communion. A communion without ecstasy. It is the necessary domain, the conversant echo—an oceanic voice when there is a dying time.

He thought of the horse he rode along the river as he woke. He woke in a blur, in his far death, farther than the old road, farther than the well-lit house he once shared, an alabaster house. He inhaled sepia ions, exhaled moss. A fire settled over the ridge. He'd seen his horse so many times—the mare's mud black hair was dull over her left eye. And her right eye, visible, blank as moth wing, as if lichen filmed her iris.

They were fading into one another, and he would lose her. He would lose The Dead as they disappeared.

It is circular, this seeing, these thin remains, projections. He scored Jupiter's mark upon the mare's flank. The shoreline's whitecaps, and Mare Undarum pointed toward the equinox. Plain ghost, his own reflection, met each ebb, from one dream to another, mother-of-pearl nights where waves swept beneath titan smog, and he would lose as his arguments remained. No glimpse of pardon, no mention. His unnamed habits were entirely original. Much of his preoccupation fell on those who resisted the agreement, and what was acquired. A presence in the danger. An incarnation of the holy within the dead ones, the dead ones within the voice of the living, upward and eternal, a belief suppressed in the madness.

Listening, The Dead sensed the first precept, reality sparked from the first fire. Love proceeding respect into a private world, faith as repentance. His eyes committed to burnt morass, a wilting deep within his gut; his not looking, not seeing. The horse would follow the first consequence, but not the first master, to follow as each stitch skipped the tear of the veil.

Her steady gaze, a protection, pushed winter's boundaries out to the sea. Symbols gleaned and sank into the wave's salt.

Her calm, complacent eyes, this companion, kicked away the buckle's edge.

Missing the tip of her ear, a huntsman's arrow rang between the pine.

When the horse lay down, he knew the foreign passage. She'd go alone, without a seacoast to follow. Bitten, in ghost fever, in a haemorrhage of flies, her throat quiet. He guarded the space, a ribboning, her breath in waves, phlegm, just half of her face, as if lifting. But she would not stand up and he thanked her. His teacher who travelled him through each province. Her way to exit, bent low, the elders passing through sand on the crest of an elsewhere village. She knew them.

He did touch the space on her neck. He did touch the arrow. He did touch the splintered bloodroot where the dust yellow moths lay. The river closes and spills from his hand. His tribe, as air, crosses the province where he, and this monk horse, now rest by the river. Drowsy his skin. Along her nape, galaxies drifted, veins sun-wobbled and sunk. He did touch a warmth. It was like a needle pulling tight the clean thread of a stitch. He did mark the black fur, the outline, the hill spur. The touch was far. And his fingers dragged the current. It was this murmur of touch arriving.

Faintly falling as she falls, a torrent of air, broadleaf, and dung. Above him the lakes on the moon shriek—loam spattered. Molecules—the limitation—shared. The limitless body. It's not true that pain is memory. He calculates his steps in his beheaded kingdom.

He never knew in advance what would happen, though he'd come close on occasion. The deer were all around him in the night. This was a seal, a silence. As careful as he can, as far from earth, now rested, now placated by this wall of etchings. Entombed, enclosed. *I am here. I am here,* in the limestone grotto above the cliff, shrouded by faded planets, upside down stags' mineral antlers, calcite stars, charcoal palm prints in limestone constellations. He travelled a thousand miles to reach this heaven.

In Centuries Later Compounding…

‡

Magdalene wrote in her ledger—

∵

Under pressure I described you, too late to reason, cottonwood's lips faded my speaking into fever.

I never broke free of the monster. I'd never follow you. But now you are in places I cannot go. My prayers are stitches in your sweat-stained garments. But I held you. And when I held you, I could see the mind's two chambers were a thousand lives, a neuropathway of consciousness incomplete and unending.

To say this is our horizon is to say the houses are now flattened. To say the nation's men drown in cigarette butts, is to say their flushed faces were purpling capillaries strewn across the grass. These fields, once a theatre of running bodies, are now dunes of poppies asleep mid-blossom. A tapestry of April's red lovers.

I remembered you were in a bed in a small hospital room at mid-day.

∴

It was Burgundy weather when the subtopic winter vines withered. In this century, the crested cockatoos were yet to be discovered, but their sulphur plumes appeared in a tapestry of the Madonna della Vittoria among the sediment, the crumbs, the warrior-saints fingering the hems of her roseate dress.

Captive now in the parade, Magdalene lived in the small dimensions: your broken sword, your plumed helmet. You too perched among winged patrons in lemon and orange trees.

‡

There was also your body. Your body had its own ideas.

She tried to stop your thoughts, but you begged her to stay with you in the room. There had already been enough revealed by your delirium. You met a messenger. You spoke of a drowned woman.

In the room of her death, when you were dying, she remembered her death. The physical world's pestilence. It raged all summer and raged all winter.

An alien substance, bacterial communication—how does energy consecrate a mediumship's awakening?

Magdalene wrote:

∴

If I could look now as if through a stereoscopic lens I would see his twisted face. The man who beat me. Somehow fate gave me that double image to reconcile myself. The self that can control the one who can't.

∴

At the fore-door, the scent of ambergris, laudanum, myrrh, and storax. In hair-shorn measure of grief's imbalance, she traded a weary glance upon the plague-doctor's glass eye, his friar's beak snivelled, his silvering buttons were a series of halos down the breast of his wool coat. Flea infected, her dress was like a flag signalling a suicidal separation from her body. She was not one for emetics, nor bloodletting, nor sips of rose hip and juniper.

A procedure was employed, a standard clinical sparing of flesh, in the assurance of miasma's surrender. She wrote:

∴

Someone is squeezing my lungs: Waterwitch, they say.

I never farewell a saint at dawn. If I am to guide The Dead, and if I am to love them, if I am to love you, who I must love as well, I must remember, and I must love—as well—in tenderness. I, as the sentiment states, hold faith in the burning city of my birth, the factory's foremen, St. Joseph the provider. Perhaps your love was my arrival. I received love unaware of your doubt, and never answered to its questions.

∴

In your delirium room she left a spell. The landlady placed a sweaty pitcher of water near the bedside hearth. Wind bit at the greased paper window. In the stifled room there was hardly any movement, but the wall trembled when you drank. In loops her cursive slumped like twisted fence lines stretching into the paddock. Her transmuted fingers rasped at complicity's silence. As if words would vilify the uninformed. The ledger continued:

∴

You may have asked how I wrote it and I understand why you called it such a loose entreaty. If you were to ask, I may have told you. But you were sombre regarding the water's musculature as you walked to the end of the sand, a scratching at birth's records, with your toe to the shore. What water was missing, a madness, milky in the dirt, like a thorn caught in a hare's throat, inhuman, a story refused, I couldn't quantify the squeal. Under pressure I described you. It was too late to reason; as your fever broke, my transmission ended.

But in this millennium, you hold the spacebar down until your finger aches and turns purple. This is what you tell me. This is how to speak without feeling the condemnation. Later you were suspicious, said my writing held an Eastern European accent. Whose ghost was at the table? How did they coerce me? Which liberty did I abandon?

This was the thing; I changed the rules as a protection from the unholy. Demonic creatures crawled in the walls and down the door frames. I heard a scurry of claws, a whisker's muffle in dust. I wrote you those letters and I imagined your response. I imagined you'd bite the buttons off my blouse, rip the seams from my pockets.

You'd be decisive that we would dump their beliefs, brush them from us or slap them to the ground like old stew. We'd hold nothing to our sides. No weapons. No relics. It's about shifting one's identity.

When I hoped for your touch, I thought of the crusades. Leaves fluttered as the round of shots dampened into your chest slipping through knots of alveoli. Your dog tag allowed for a small dent on the right side of your name. I never asked about the history of the religion which felled you. I never prayed under its reign.

In particular trades there is a physical toll.

∴

Abruptly, yet still gently, she brushed off the forest air. Half-awake, her hands warmed the half-ruddy skin on his left cheek where he'd slept against her chest. They were alone now.

And at the forest edge, drunk soldiers stood. The crawl space between one mind and the other, just less than three feet wide, was a perfect calm through which she might stumble. Yes, she stumbled off into the other dimension, the next life, as she became bold, and unfolded into the centre of the sniper's gun. He thought quickly, and how quick it was to take the living out of the body. Quick always were unjust actions, the pre-crimes, the post-crimes. She'd been, for this while, the one to survive amnesty's possession. But now she knelt over a flat body. Her body, which lay flat under the flat insistence of rain. She lay in the space now without a child. She lay her infant beside her still living body. She streamed between strangers, and held them where they waited, the double current where the unsung are kept.

In every cell, in the line of sight as her first line, she at once made peace to it, *sweet body. My body I lay and lay in him too. I, in dream to you—*

And he, dreaming a woman he would never see.

The nature of mercy gives hold into the unseen, *where my horse, my horse with dying eye, my dead-eyed horse*

Yes, it is very sweet, the body once it has found peace, purer into the unseen where she thought her loved ones were looking. In the molecular night, a spirit provoked an energy from the body, her body, hidden in grass thickets. A widow's throat shut out the whisperings, the trees chattering, as if she was guided into a small room.

ON THE PLAINS OF ABRAHAM

Death Speaks:

▽

I strung a gull's talon in my hair, and a passerine's dried heart hung from my waist in a rabbit skin satchel. I never spoke into him. And he followed me. In the trail of my declination there was a blindness by which I came back to him.

I stare now as if staring into an injury. I, the injury. He held me hard and gave one bite below my breast.

There was a cabin and a wooded space. The name I wouldn't tell. I planted myself small into the room. Walls of cherry trees in rows where the foreigners planted milk-scarlet blossoms. If now I could close my eye to the great sun, it might be practical.

It was the first death, and the only in the sixth season of loss. You were my second, and only living, a son bonded to my magic, the shift complete. I found your body. You lay in the scorched field far from the sea's washup, black feathers spread through the needle grass. In my last instinct, I held you in your sling, reached for the bauble, and the bell, and the jay's feather. I fingered the red lard from your brow, pressed a crimson smear to my lip. What was it to show my feeling when no fault is held within your soft sleep. On the last morning of our world, I washed your hands, your feet, your arms. I remember the western ravens, a pretence of rain, an agate liquid flooded our skin, we faded from one another. They bound me as I stood over your body.

I saw myself imprinted. Black eyes hollow against the charred field, I stood before your body haloed in salt crust. The horse of the first horse, speared, and held to the ground where we fell. Rain-washed and mud-clogged, sudden saplings unfolded up under your hair. Your eyes flagged. Two sails. An emblem sent through my lungs. The sea washed through you until what was dry opened to the wet, slick as sea kelp.

I watched a small girl drive out the vultures and thaw mice from the blankets. I left her my straw-yellow dress. I set the air right. A curtain swept across the plains.

She would never answer to the land, to the unspoken actions. The field resolved her conception. She took it. She took it just as she'd always taken the earth as a dedication. When she was punished, when the soldier circled her, this new eclipse, an opening through which to survive the violence, she embodied the survival of violence.

His actions were of no concern. It was no concern of hers, the imperfection, the intestinal longing. When the raid came, she dry-wretched into the sand. The wound came and the wound deepened, and she held the wound as if holding a basket. There was no domain. There was no home. It wasn't her place anymore. And there was no place else to go. So, she went under.

In the long hours before it first started, the horses clung to the clearing where she was found. The mare paced the blue clay, felt a quickening up through the wet sand into her mouth.

After the soldiers left, she'd been the one who stood. The one who stood and stared into the end of a shotgun. But this sequence was a reversal.

∆

The Dead: Today, Hereafter, Yesterday

‡

Magdalene tells The Dead to come to the table, the pool hall, the community dance.

The echo of the future heightens as they pass. In what and where she exists, they do not hear.

She'd taken to the small house, to the williwaw, to the Christmas lagoon. But the sun didn't track well on the horizon. A hair tangled the page. A bracken around the notebook hardened. Her mark making was a loose order. She thought of it quite often. She thought of the hard line they rode. She thought of him beneath the earth. She turned the paper over. She crossed out the dun-coloured grass, the hawthorns, the ibis. His margin held her margin. One inaudible pattern calls to the other. Her arms, spokes of a wheel, tip her fingers into curves and ragged dashes, into vaporous sparrows and arrows and scrawls. The earth spins on in solitude. A line appears. It bends as she moves through it. It leaves. He leaves. She still speaks to him often. He says the people of his city are immortal. He says ash by ash, the old language becomes the first.

If you love a certain shadow, please love mine, she says.

What Magdalene never meant to say fell to the open river. Sometimes he became someone she recognized.

She lost her family in the raid. She never declared her injury. In atonement, consciousness would be observed. Their limits, visible now, the canyon's imperfection—their bodies lay in the glen past the grinding stone. He'd saved her against artillery—

spared the massacre. She never reached the tower at the fort. They travelled south where the snow splintered the river and deer froze deep in mud.

She lowered the dead into place—there was no other cultivation. The bloodroot failed, a salve upon the tongue of each small life. They died together with their words. The light going out, the evening a spell.

She would start from what rescue held in her. She wanted to leave, to follow the river, and return to the small house. She wanted to measure what remained to measure. There was a sodden forest half a mile beyond the city from where she came, where the orchard grasses bent into the patch of green. The horses were gone and a few cows, like a vow, lingered in the open mud. She didn't say their names with softness, she didn't say their names. Blossoms became their figures in the open rain.

‡

You stole the vaquero's horse, pulled a blanket and rifle off the dead soldier, emptied his canteen over your face. You slipped past the sentinel as he stood at the ridge under the cedar. It may have been daylight, but there was no sun. There was a sound of a shot or the sound of an arrow. Or the sound of sun spinning in two directions. It was the sound of someone saying your name, but you couldn't hear them. The sun going down. The sun not yet risen. You arrive slowly. Your horse steps forward and will not back over the bodies. There is a scar-trail space the fires stripped. Halfway down the lane the horse eyes the distance, then leans, a horse, running toward flames, dusk horse, and lantern. All that goes, goes with it. It is all that goes with that.

Province to Province…

∴

> *At the river we anointed our foreheads with salt. Later, under the bridge we lay in silence. You didn't feel my kindness, nor discriminate against my motives. I held your palms open against mine. In a four handed prayer we mumbled a false decree as The Dead surrounded us measuring our words. Walls of apology opened; rain evaporated on our cheeks as noon rose above us. This was the ritual we made of love —*

∴

For years Magdalene dreamed that a still grey battlefield stretched before her, a foreknowledge—its precise effect—an invisible wound. She couldn't correct what he thought of her. Her language folded; as did the first man or the first woman's obsolescence as victor. She as kill code. It was the moment her body's injury created an interior, as if she became another country, one kicked at the centre. This is when she lost her language. What she believed was taken from her, into him, was only an unprotected sheltering, a spiritual dispersal.

She surrendered without consciousness. Once she'd given, and once she believed what she'd given was taken, only then did possession take hold. A subterranean thought-form, not a philanthropic demarcation, but a survival-level transmission. A plover's nest scratched into the gravel is not a nest at all, but an instinct in camouflage. As within her, her wound stood upright, or floated as a sentient being, separate from her body, nucleic, parasitic. Her wound, like a banner or an appendage. But her wound was only the belief held by the living who said she was dead. Some people called this limbo, but the truth is that only the living believe you are not alive.

In aberrant moments, she clawed at her scar, a gash above her left eyebrow. The sudden weakness, her own cat's claw scratching at her eye, was beyond her control. She perceived remote visions. She dreamed he came to her that night, where they met at the outskirts of town, under the deserted half-edges and cinder-block rubble. She sensed a camera upon her in her sleep as she led him by his wrist down a spill of damaged walkways. She knew of a little school desk in the hovel below the dam, and next to it, half a piano keyboard smashed by the riverbank.

Crossing the town's bridge, her throat surged. Under the hardwood battens, the birds gathered like a bridegroom might abide marriage, lustreless as a prison cell, sheltering in the corner. She felt the swallow's scapulars and mantle at the nape of her neck as they bore anchorage into the exuberant dark. A muscular pressure up her spine eased as their wings fluttered and they flew past to nest in ship hulls. On this night, fire deflected the wash-up of maggot-fleshed fish. To spite death, to avoid binding, those officers kept a handful of lovers, kept themselves wholly private, and when The Guards came, and when the execution arrived, they held silent above the sound of the shooting.

Without a known face, she loved this soldier; his Christmas voice rose above the others. A choral forgiveness among the spears and reeds.

∴

I am not sure how this happens, but I believe it can. Right now, I hear a car door shut and footsteps on the gravel. This may seem vague to those who have not heard this sound but because I am familiar with sensation, I understand the pattern. Perhaps it is something like this, and then my imagination rises from instinct to know if the postmistress or a relation with violent red hair is picking up a potted plant or delivering a postcard. Or is it my tall husband arriving home from the grocer. Blanks I can fill in but these to me are mundane not the incubation I desire to feed. I am hopeful to be led by an inner monster unperturbed by the outer world of which I am no longer part, except as shadow—I cannot see, except as shadow, I cannot see, despite my awareness for what is. Luck is that someone may understand my choice to feed the outer sea-dragons. Later we may call it a dugong, a dolphin, less likely a shark, more fortunate perhaps an octopus, sawfish, eel, crown of thorns.

∴

Hereafter, Hereafter

Death Speaks:

▽

I have left you and what I've left of you is mixed in me. I am learning to cease the ritual of confession. People drift apart. It doesn't need to be a nightmare. A sunset is casual, peace can be petitioned. A pennant of tenderness arches over the grass.

Tiger snakes blacken into ebony where the land is cold. This is not animal myth. The elder recorded fossils when they dredged the lagoon. Long after, we discovered a rib bone. Hard as a rock, free of sediment. What is worse, a selflessness close to failure. Or what shows itself. We were never scavengers.

On the battleground I knew you were not my love. Also, I knew the earth as a house I could not love, but I entered anyway. I polished the crevasse, your silence I could understand. When I leaned into the scent of pine, ammonia, the barely sound of bells ringing through the mop, through my hands, I felt flat: the ocean a smooth page. Yes, I am glad. In the battlefield dreams I see the chapter written with moss. You are not mine. You are not an other. I love you in this way directly as if we fight together. Not against the tide. On a day easy as a routine adventure.

I fed you what I could bear to feed. I have given you my body for burning. I have given you the transparent bodies, a glimpse of your face in the glass. The Dead are desperate with desire. The Dead are poking your heart with needles.

I am traveling toward the crooked shore where your hand is a precipice. I sent you a sketch of my face on a tattered post-it note.

There is a luxury in being left. In being the one considered remnant.

Δ

As the shelling began

‡

It wasn't the sun, but a lily—the rays of Madonna's heart spread beyond the ocean—no Pleiades grid, not a generic death—he, a dagger like waves, rows his boat through dawn's tunnel, red war kerchief knotted at his throat, and surrender's white rag: a tourniquet strapped numb to his shin as the king tide breaks seawall to clay.

He leans into the coordinates, north as longing.

Still, beneath the water's wake, he senses you, who he buried without a map, a stone as your spine mimics a sandbar's profile, undulations a shallow whip.

He touched his scar. He touched his father's death bullet, shrapnel hole, clovis point—he imagines your eyes when his father was close to ruin.

He, an Unnamed Soldier. One left behind. One fell behind. One who faced the attack. Or retreated. Deflated by protections. He protects his own vigilance. Walks with vigilance in dedication of each command. Now, he is a recurrent gravity in the state of this elegy, but every war is a state of elegy. He is recursion. Someone comfortless. An anti-hero, a bystander, citizen of the imperative empire. He is the one, who through wound, would no longer be wounded. Who would no longer be wound.

The bodies brought home were still homeless. O this close you understand the flame as confession…

you didn't like the tiny cracks like stars stained on his teeth or the sand's anchorage in his hairline or the sidewalk upon which plastic telephones once clicked among glass and metal booths.... you didn't like the past... you didn't like the thought of The Dead, nor he, the missing among them...

You didn't like that he was thinking of you as a saviour. You didn't like it that in the battle he found you in the small trench; he found you alone like a second spirit; his companions turned their backs, as your commands settled like carbon all around them.

‡

Da Nang Outpost, 1969

You told him you would think of him as he disappeared deep into country. You would think on that day he sought you in the heaviest attack. The battalion's dogs were airlifted with the troops as the enemies advanced, but many dogs died of heat exhaustion, their heads heavy on the chest of the unconscious men.

‡

All Negotiators turned a slow blade into the slowly shadowed earth, muzzled into a flame beyond the river, earth the churning soil into body and water. There are several forms of survival. You would meet them. You would curl against the shelter. You would look for yourself. You would look for the substance of terror. The pinprick, Titan's citrine haze. Twilit sleep. From your half open mouth, ravens appeared as a warning. A blot on the horizon. You spoke: your voice, a clean undertow, as rumour, flooded the landscape. You never named your intention. You never understood you were already dead.

Each morning, more alleyways were bombed. Smoke held in your hands, like a lathe turning— You held smoke. Your hands streaked in gunpowder; you held the enemy's return. They marched as you loaded the cannons. You wanted to name this. You wanted to name this as a condition. These were not terms of surrender, but incarnations, prehistoric visions of you, dimensions sent without warning. This grip, a flashback, a plasma that rushed cold down your spine. Swamp water slithered up through your stomach, a blackout reaching your senses. You didn't know how yet, but this was love. A love twisted out—weeds from ruins and roots of prior despair.

Before the war, there was the scent of war. There was a third lung filled with decay, filled with dust and flake of sparrow's wing. The sea bird's disappearance was a premonition that shadowed the channel. Naval ships loomed like new cities on the horizon.

‡

Among the dusky sea sparrows

You didn't know if it was the birds or an apotheosis. There is no language to deal methodically with emotional bias. Too threatening, words don't follow understanding and thoughts remain hidden in a box which holds belief into factual states of light. It is a slideshow of images, a green mountain, glass the sky is upon—a softening voice in subtitles. Occasionally the view switches to another person, a book of pressed seaweed, a midnight satellite, or an unfamiliar room.

You threw yourself in the water, merciless and slow against the deep. Magdalene recorded your swim through shallow reefs. Seaweed fingered your sternum. Your arm's limber strokes wove a cold surge as you crossed the currents to reach the shore where at last you stood in the alternate atmosphere. At a makeshift kitchenette without walls, you peeled potatoes at the sink.

She churned in your dream, she, of your first beginnings.

You remember your name in various tones. A kind of practice. Yes. You remember your death; You remember your birth. You'd swum through the afterlife.

You never believed in superliminal communication, this telepathy where she held you in the wake of your body's air and sand plugs your throat.

She lived with you, but you could not look eye in eye; you lived beyond the dimension where touch is a tedious matter, and the perceptions of touch give spiritual crafting.

In this stone house, you spurred the ritual. Elphin bones bordered the garden all the way down as salt dusted the gulch. Magdalene told you—*the border's cleared.* You noted her manifestos, marginalia tagged in sun faded ink on the ledger paper, now streaked with green welcoming horizon lines— ditched as some transient slag, shoved in a tote-bag between three-month's breakfast and bedtime. You scraped a backdrop: a cockcrow over dryline over eucalypt beyond palm, but she pointed up to the vine strangling tree fern. Now only steam gathered in the boiling pot. Your glasses clouded. You held no courage to meet her eyes in your strange parallel. It is a willingness to oust the question. And to wade into a river. To invoke together what The Dead concealed. To strengthen two worlds in fellowship is to look her in the teeth: at first abalone, pearly, but the aperture of her mouth was narrow.

She walks between the tree's double negatives, in the banded shade between jacarandas where the atmosphere is a channel to the outer world. As by turns, your instruments equate to failure. Yes, you're held open to the question. No option but to wait. The North Sea flags. Her earlier death conceded and so she is stitched into seamlessness and lays deep beneath the sun. When she constructed the second message there was no more ledger. You were very sick by then. You never wanted to die. She said—

Did I tell you? The streets in this section are candlelit. I'm no longer conditioned by a view for leaving. They've given me some land. I plant iris along the boundary now to disembody my own form. The she-oak and sycamore reach up through my limbs and are an almost-pleasure unsated. The windows warp in the heat. The crickets scratch a new morse code. At night, I leave my door ajar.

The house in summer felt small and looming. The humidity broke our mouths wide open with salt. We touched each word. Our mouths, the hollow eye of a fish; The Dead spoke through us without language. You, among The Dead, did not die in your dying.

The foresun closes her domestic door. You ask her if you are in a trance. You say you are protected by a message. The Dead appear in a medium unknown by spells. They are left to remind you. It was danger, the earth, a demon you remembered, your touch and untouch, a trinity in the wavelengths.

Someone whispers across the apple orchard. Someone touches her. Someone who is nothing real. *It is helpful to have you here,* Magdalene says, at last, when healing lands a deeper turn. Someone is buried in this naming.

No one would come near because she was dying. There is a lucidity that erases touch—like the intentions of a witch coven tromping through her sleep, an inertia drawing you in, drawing you over ice, over an angled bridge, over the moment the cold house becomes the last flame of ochre in the autumn woods, a char in the mind. The loss that is never a loss because you remember it. Remember, the ambient environment changes when we are physically in love.

There was no need for family gifts. Her years had been long, and she came to embrace certain genetic mysteries. A leafy airiness and a lilac's ambrosia carried her. She could accept the slope of a visitant's dim shadow around her. She would dwell easily in the ancestral realms knowing the dark was sourced from the brightest light.

She knew and understood the soliloquy of her body, but the rituals of comfort, the ones created to soothe her body after her mother's death, to soothe your grief, were denied.

Death Speaks:

∇

In an empty room, I fitted an ampoule of hemlock beneath my armour. The terms of my condition were seemly in the hour by which to vindicate authority. I didn't know the path where the charred driftwood opened upon the sea's surface, the channel through which your voice might return. I didn't know failure nor contrition.

I was met among the prophets, anonymous, anointed, a seeker. I was assigned time's geologic course. The heat of my body would be short-lived. And I heard only in the moment what my guide provided—a diagram, a leaching of earth's interior. What did he say, how to yield, what was not said. I relished the taste of our language.

And here is the thing about those nights. One minute, in oath, cranes lifted above the estuary, and our munitions embroidered the anonymous country. We hid momentarily between the screen of sumac leaves in the air's thrum—a silver highway of wings. The next moment, a seraph in the tight azure above pressured the bird's formation against the scarlet orbs of Orion.

Did I go wool-gathering or less remember my conversion. I held no foresight. Soaked by groundwater, I rest in a bed of chamber-grass under the buzz of crickets and dampened tanker's impending plough. The mangrove was a pact between enemies who soundlessly arrived upon it.

There was no inventory of my faults. In hell's precinct I broke the last heel of bread, held your wrist, a pulse of bacon rind.

A pangolin's scale upon your eye, your face a fresh loam. You were carted into the sweep of survivors who didn't survive. No blessing. No arrest.

Far along the town's bombardment all the sleeping casualties remained. A spackle of flies beset the earth's depression of caribou antlers, and each pile of warriors splayed across the ravine became a phrase, a new effort of dialect. Scores of sparrowhawks pressured skylight's dome. The echo of drums in the reeds was a wormhole to the other territory.

My new formula for grief: who might survive, and who, with hammer, might crucify.

I love both illusions: those who ebb out of the trees in a single paradigm as a formless, spectral lucidity among magnolia leaves, and those whom I am meant to hate.

I was an apprentice to chance. I was immune to what caution left me.

Yes, in the pre-dark of that century, the night I dreamed you, we spoke in reversals. The immodest horizon held no desire.

And I woke with blood smeared on my white skirt and raw lips. And this was after a line of men one by one entered the chevy, sharing the blow-up doll within my body. And faithless, I floated upward to the saints who brandished their needles and popped each star.

We met drowning in a hotel room. Liquor filled my lungs, almost choking in sleep before I reached mid-ocean. No way to find our way toward. We swam miles to the last vessel.

Tide's haemorrhage was our captor. I lived in the awareness of the trawl: arms and fins and scales and hair.

I can tell you I am almost known among the stuffed figures of the endangered—godwit, thylacine, vaquita—in scientific descriptions a bang of my obsidian-capped teeth are a dissolution of the constellations.

Now the eyes of the aurochs are only tertiary colors in the physical realm.

Δ

Magdalene's ledger noted—

∴

When your body was left among shags of wild crabgrass, I loosened my hair and reflected on your hands crossed over your grey wool suit, your tie balancing your heart, your new silence.

I wondered for a while if I'd been viewing the scene through the window of a train. I saw ordered rows. Read the sky's vertigo. Years shining up like eyes through verdigris plains. By morning the sun's wide desire and the under-wing of a grosbeak greeted indigo streaks of soil. Noon ended the real mind. Still, I think of you as if you might return. Then I remembered that view: autumn's contractions expelling the last stubborn leaves from the oak, the field dizzy with dusk weather.

∴

‡

You want you to enter your body, ghost returned from ghost, to enter the grass on which The Dead are standing. You want The Dead to rise up under you and be seen.

I'm not certain, but sometimes intuition fades, you tell them. But they are not encouraged.

You think about how trauma enters the body. It is like water entering a swimmer until the water permeates every cell, and particle by particle, the swimmer and the ocean hold one another. You think about this unfolding as a strange compassion and how you are estranged from yourself. In this moment of awakening, intimacy is a bridge. There is a time for this, as love's evolution lifts out of the soil, bodily, without denial, and finds domain—but it is not a physical existence. It is a boat at the edge of a black lake where we gather to row through the night.

‡

For a time, you had a language. Soil, silt, the means by which we'd spoken. Death's voice a pressure through the waterways *and I let the river tire you.* Reeds rim the banks, a meadow nearby, or far away, lifted. *Twice I could say the waters took me,* Death's hum: as revenant luck or a vanishing bitter god. Acts of creation, translation, or control. You pressed seaweed between your thumbs, laid each specimen flat upon the sun blanched boulder. You ran your fingers down algae spines. Then, sample by sample, you rolled each pattern into hessian cloth. You layered the kelp samples, like a small thieving, into your basket.

The leather-bound book of seaweed and a box of ash were held in the glass collector's cabinet. You felt the hills, a tumult toward you, lifting. The earth and the ocean were held beneath glass, a corridor in which you were made to wait. The air around you, like a fist, was a thud coming down.

As the science of earth bites down, we chew upon our own decay.

Now it's too late for everything. It was midnight. You remembered yourself as a soldier. You remembered the soldier trapped in the tank. You remembered the tank burning.

You set up the camera in her room and she fed it your reflection.

You pulled out the box of photos and pamphlets with faces and palm trees.

There it was in your body. A great fire. As if your body was thrown from the car as you skidded off the road, and you had left something behind.

An admission slid through your lips in your old projections, either from your identity, or from the moment of necessity. In the dream you seemed younger than the time before.

A dying time. Who am I in damage. What have I done, you said.

What is sacred cannot be nourished. It is a glimmer. This is a form of time.

A truth: the domain of your death is the easiest hour. All the courage you could believe, the attack of the body on the easiest day. The intimacy of this language flees, and shadow can be seen. You read these things. You entered the gate. There is a time to deny the language once written so that the intimacy of this language flees and shadows emerge.

Magdalene wanted to be like the others. To be like the others and fall into trance to forget. To forget and write in the ledger: *In a passageway I stopped once, turned as if to follow you out, but the shootings continued. You told me I would know the field where you stood.*

The machine guns were left facing the target. Only one landmine spat out an elliptical cloud, which spread from a triangular blast, as if a portal opened above each of the women and children. Each instantaneous grave floated. Each, an omen.

When I think of violence, I see your capacity to kill, she noted in her ledger. *Something of your other lovers remained. You cradled their qualities. Their remnants sustained you in lush communications. It was strange, always, but useful for the things I now understand.*

She emptied herself as you emptied yourself. She keyed in on phrases from The Dead but took no note of you. She took no note of her own will. You assumed a certain love within yourself existed, a love for the masses of dead to maintain in the love for the living. And you knew it would never turn out. For each of The Dead, once at the extreme of their lives, felt the curious realms devoured them.

It seemed several times you dropped your guard. Yes, your guard dropped, and you learned these things about The Dead. You no longer saw through double vision. All outer and all inner worlds withdrew across the line of vanquished strangers. No more illusion, you saw god beyond each fallen consciousness.

In precision, the battalions returned from battle. Inside the night, in onyx camouflage, they watched a planetary retrograde. Water was now a human ointment. Simultaneously such waters, now human waters.

They kept hidden your entry. You crept away from the trenches as tactic. You crouched and you waited.

You waited to gather tinctures, to blood-let the enemies' wounds. It was an exchange. And you took it. You saw skin breaking, saw the landscape's adaptation. Nothing seemed unfair in this combustion.

A series of voices projected again and again in echo. Magdalene noted the words of The Dead and translated these in her book. The Dead's thoughts intermingled with her own thoughts, not conversant but mixed, as in a tidepool at the cliffs of the Opal Coast, or in muddied pits beneath Messines Ridge:

∴

The city was the distance between me and the bombsite.

You'd been the one for which I was saving a single word.

I love the nature of you, love the bloom in you. I love the nature of the bloom in you.

I came to you now with my whole body opening to see.

I found no other name for this desire, but I believed in loveliness. I believed in the revisionist's approach to time.

By degrees, your role as witness was my interrogation. Yes, it was almost a dare. What I gambled. Complacency levels your face. I believe your eyes now are an absolute masquerade. Clandestine, one small dilution into one small dilution. Every true being might imagine you. I saw you, and once thought you were real.

If anyone came, I would go mad. And assuming we could not escape, I'd want you to leave my body behind.

In fact, every morning I wanted to leave my body. The same way you'd left yours. I am slowly and privately escaping. I was private in my alien fears. Perhaps they'd think I am dead, but I am alive. Night's knowledge becomes the dreaming. It is the only way. It is the only real explosion. The bombing rediscovered, without doubt, the city—a giant furnace to keep the body electric. I have said it many nights, just as you, I am alive among The Dead.

∴

Grey light across the valley shifted into cobalt. Solitude was never yours. Unbidden, you are not the other to whom The Dead travelled. You wanted to declare every distant sun, until all but one of The Dead disappeared and the horizon went blank. In the opposition of planets, you stood. In one direction, Jupiter; in the other, the moon's Mare Imbrium.

You were disturbed by the tonic of silence. At the face of it, it seemed The Dead lived within insomnia's fragments, a habitable world where they took solace in the repetitious feeling of loneliness.

Magdalene records what passes, your permanent lapses, your words, and your wonder. There were fragments of self, quivering in despondence, arriving late with optimism.

The charcoal landscape fractures the river's pebbled reflection like a rip on a missing woman's sleeve. Embroidered yellow florets stretched through the arroyo and up the ravine. A witchery swept across greasy grass and the sand's stretchmarks. With her claybark skin, cat-black hair, her lips—in a vascular spill of vervain, Magdalene broke open the soldier's wound.

Sea-lice swelled in her veins, a secret anima. Her arms, a bed of subterranean waves.

She showed you the granite edges of the sea, the red moss along eucalyptus scented river.

What chance is there? you asked.

In my current location? Slim, she replied.

‡

Today, Yesterday, After Her Death

Death Speaks:

▽

There were star points and if you drew them back through the water, they were planetary and smooth like the men's eyes, like marbles cold in her mouth.

As I walked from the island's radar station up to the lighthouse, you remembered Magdalene. I also remembered her, though I did not know her. She died, directionless as her body drifted to Michealmas Cay, no thanks to a map. Now she is just clickings—crystal ribs and pelvis bones, sand, glass, and coral. She is the sound of chimes. She is the clarity of other realms in wave's circuitry. She'd travel among tides to observe time's mixed tyrannies.

She was bound by a great thing: the love to love you, and now to love you without form. That voice, her voice within waters and groves, shaken from streams, eddying the last lake, she is the voice of imperfect stars. Under the sight of green Neptune, you leaned over the horizon, a window to which you are carefully tethered. The shadows of the sea were weary. The snow is now thick under the dense sky. The scent of cedar balms the hills. We will go one into another, into the shade of the woods and chase the wild horses through the scrub.

She senses you now only as sound. The sound of your old voice, a stasis within the sea, a static, a tape-recorded dial tone, a tremulous whoosh, wave's articulation against the tide. There is one dimension only. And light damages the object of the sea. And the sea relents, carrying flashes of your terror, a deep whirl, so as if beneath your skin, impermeable, fear like water, is diluted and uncertain. A condition like each condition, terrestrial.

Yes, you will go, one into another, swaying back and forth— her hair shifts as seaweed. Reeds amass in a tributary. The fingerling shore stretches under the base of a dome. There is a great tide at noon that stables the body. What was it before us, as if the earth is skinned and an emptiness leaks up. A green lantern sinks beneath her. The sea was pre-arranged. Just as the other hemisphere shapes the hour, pauses, then sinks her.

Δ

‡

Betrayal lives in the betrayed

You had a hand in your own failures. To be alive is to be of injury. The meadow heaves, and the wind in slow degrees wakes the will of your language. It is an old language, wordless in injury, as you are wordlessness among them: caught among The Dead and the dead languages. And in injury, the American soldiers surrounded you, the injured. And, as in a movement of language, the wheels and the spokes of language, a language of lack in which you were attacked for speaking, your voices travelled as a stream. A blue shimmering rose above your enemy. Every silence was a crime under the wheel. Every wheel descended through the shivering trees as the will of language, your code. This non-speaking is your breath as the body gives way. You were going there. Snow soothes the eddies, and the river disappears among the cowslips, the bluebunch, the bush rue. You move the body of your language forward as the ice thaws. The will and your courage of will. To move language forward is not a light endeavour. Not without politic. You have said this again and again and you will say it again and again. Even if it is only to yourself that you speak. But there is always a lack of justice in the communion of will. You regret your observations, the time and distance it takes to unfold your progression. You regret this pity.

These things are past. But there were times you blamed yourself. No one could see your face from the outside, the silent arrival of the basalt canyon into new plains. In dreams there was a valley in which people lived. It was an agony. There was a lake at the bottom of the ravine flooded by storm-birds. There was a proper bruise across your country, burbling fallows, a soft dissolving of the foals into salt flats. You rested under the splintered rifles, without atonement, the last inhabitants. True or untrue. You believed in no such thing as beauty. Nor winter's hesitations. The buck's antlers spread across the field like fingers reaching upward against disease or danger.

An elder woman appeared after the downpour, surrounded by her daughter and grandchildren. She told you her illness was without pain. You told her you would help.

Perhaps you will explain, she said.

She told you earlier that day not to trust anyone and told you plain the symbols of distance: a geometry of ants up the boulders, bread broken by ashen mouths. A woman of two rivers was this woman's warning in indigo diagrams, the coordinates and loops like after patterns of wildfire. This was your last terrain.

You never knew the way to it, toward this mind within your mind. But more deeply you lay beneath the trees, counted the birds, and wrote your way. And what you wrote brushes across the arbour. Each bird, a mirror, a mercy you could nourish. Each bird, a yellow sail, a unity of flight, a legend like the sun. Each bird, a song, held within its own shadow. You hiss in your repose.

‡

Now the Sorrel stands in the ditch-dirt. Spring shifts. Snow trickles at his hooves. You cross the valley of weeds as he teeters between patches of buckthorn and saltwort. He comes with you. He travels the waypoints. He comes, as if your admission called him. He just comes.

WORLD WAR I

Hotel Trianon, Hospital, Le Tréport, 1914

From the hospital window on the cliffs above town, you saw the roof smeared in cinder flakes. Anthracite hour, the smell of anise burning, the dark going out over the Bresle estuary. Nothing left, your legs a failure.

In sickness, in a lie, with one clean hand holding the ghost at the door, and with one hand deep into the press of the horizon, a person can change. Snow can rip or unzip the sky like a tarp. Someone can call you home, can speak in suddenness like headlamps passing between the trees. A person can lie down, either in peace or in anguish or both, and in full desire of it all, not get up. When The Doctor packed your wound, two messages aligned. You were overtaken, or would be soon, and you must be willing. You couldn't lift yourself. The sun burned the window each morning. In duplicity, you perfected a state of gladness. Your social psyche, the better twin, fingered the gash along your jawline. It remembered the body's interface with matter. It allowed you to change form as the environment adjusted to trauma.

At the flywire window, a tear appeared, a slash line rather like a worm hole through to another body. Contained there surely, was the theosophy of other lives. Instead, there appeared an altar where the Madonna's face arrived. Our Lady of Power in symbol and language. In flaming crimson robes, harvest fires, a kindling of brush and wet chafes of wheat. Centuries of snakes crawled up her thighs.

You stare through a strange smear of oil on the window, the shape of an Irukandji, only yellow. You wonder about the difference between strength and decay's resistance. Unlike the moment you laughed and, in a circle of sawdust, saw the imprint of your boot in the realm of the living. Yes, the sun vanishes for a minute at midday. The cobalt eye of the blazed mare opens in your somnambulism. You follow her path between two archways. Someone said the sun is coming back, but the year is fading.

She sat on your shoulder in the other sphere. Two intersections settled. She said you were a player in the creation.

She said: *I'll come back. I'll come in numerous apparitions. And walk into the room, soundless.*

The Great Retreat 1914

‡

Bales of hay are spread through the town square where the French soldiers rest in the plaza after a march. Rows of horses and men lower among the lingering dust, crowded among packs and munitions. The streets and shops are closed.

Magdalene stares at this photo and thinks how the women did not exist. The women did not exist. The women left the town in which they lived. When the men came, the women left for the seaport fifteen miles away without discussion. Of course, the children and the elderly left too. Their exodus was a new language of the era. Their disappearance had come to the townspeople and the soldiers knew how this happens. No one spoke of it or why.

The town was dirty and smelled like rot. The Translator fingered the breadcrumbs on the kitchen tables. Glasses of water glowed on the nightstands. A body of warmth remained. A scrapbook lay singed beneath the morning light; a photo album splayed in the rubble along with a pair of wire rim reading glasses.

The light from an east window is always sacred.

The twice travelled night closed over the sleeping village.

At some point the men would walk into the open landscape and the horses would walk behind them, upslope in the heat. Under the open air they would lay in an encampment without tents.

‡

Magdalene wondered about the men. They were good men, and it was a tireless job, this human migration from place to place, this "othering" which occurs, which must occur. She made a wish for love without thinking.

Her wish for love was certainly love in certainty. Desire, as a certainty, shapes healing. This wish might settle between their shoulder blades. Her wish, which was a prayer, was rust-coloured dirt that spread between the men as they lay at night, in the open. A tarnish grew between them. A stain grew between the men, a thick scar, and this blemish stretched outward to the sea's edge.

In an arid haunting over a thousand terrains, over the eastern front, over the western front, diagrams pinned duress as location. The map marked a sovereign landscape where the lease was paid in advance. The debt solidarity conceives, an openness to loss, irreconcilable and ancient. Truth healed only in reflection. Why would the women resist. After a time, closer and closer, the remote desert crept nearer to them. At the marina, the wind in the mast flowered into the sound of a distant bell. The women dream a slow wound. A halo breaks the horizon wide. An impersonal failure begins. The women accepted the sea, accepted the make-shift shanties as spaces of prostration.

Some think it impossible to be hard, to be uneven. Some think that *what happens to you will not happen to me* because each experience is limitless. You are an assassin to your own measures. You measured the light. But when you think of it, when you think of the light, it's fair to say that light assumes its place. And it is fair enough to promise that an attraction to the earth exists. And the earth, briefly gives, but in counterturn, folds a devastation toward you. Meanwhile, the earth exalts the spirit. And in your mind, you must say, there were pleasant effects, the light, a yellow soot, ochre yarrow, like the centre of the soldier's lips.

The city in which the women lived was an incomplete sketch. Years later, the women made drawings of the town and thought of home. The place from a long time before, now on their deathbeds, was remembered.

‡

Without speaking, the soldiers rode the horses in the desert during the war. Through El Arish, Raffa, Magdhaba, Beersheba, they travelled always further. Behind their backs the ocean shrugged. Each wave, a salve, a dank promise of indifference and humility.

Trainlines embroidered the Sinai desert.

Yes, soon there were trains which led them away. Soon there were piles of bones outside the city.

The liberties of the next generation were a freedom conceived close within the city the women fled; they did not want; they did not feel your want. They were gathered in the one place. Sashes, like clauses in an agreement, they followed, assigned to each exception, as the soldier's travelled hope's shredded ribbons. In Egypt, the villagers stacked loaves of bread on the tarp for the soldiers, and the mud ovens, like shallow trenches, prophetic. The faces of the villagers peered in from the outer courtyard traced with red shadow. Motionless, the houses burned, the transit centres and the prisons filled. The interrogation was a discordant list of names. Sudden assault, sudden darkness—the soldiers, the circumstance, the climates that eventuate.

A war is a merging and an emergence. A war is a pact in time which carries each person's history forward slightly deeper. It is a luxury of the future. It is a naive heat that closes one's throat while sleeping.

In distance, in distracted thoughts, an old officer led the soldiers to a high plateau where the nature of beauty would be exposed. On the hill, in the open, and all through the edge of that town which they passed months earlier, he'd thought of a semi-perfect number, a semi-perfect spring blossom, the apple trees in bloom, the orchard after a late snow. The landscape was luminous even as the squadron cleared the chamois and led the goats over the hill.

Magdalene's hair was now a patch of Lenten roses across the woodland floor.

There is an insular rule which slips her back into the loop—just as the sun rose, and just as the sun set, the infinity returns them to the same position.

Everything came into view. The world asleep; no light of the old traditions within it now. The earth above. Wordless. Magdalene dropped formalities. You both dropped through atmospheric miles. She touched the shape within the light which excised each darkness. You woke with the bell. And you ended the bell. You died under the ringing.

You loved three words hidden within the ledger: *Kindness is Victory.* You loved the greenery and the groves which you might touch. You did not lose the embodiment, the physical body's first sharpness.

You stand in her room at night and watch her breathe. The gloam covers the grove and the group of The Dead that surround her.

The pages of the ledger distract you. You've cracked open the binding into the escape. Opened into love. There is a blaze at the edge of the star picket fence in the west corner of the pasture. An osprey passes just as the night slips upward—he is the riding of light along the rail. You ride the light upward, upward to see yourself. A self-unnamed, a self-unknown—a faceless conscience, a ceaseless warrior. You step out from the page. Shade beneath shade spreads out from the elm where you stood. Your grey wool coat shimmers with spring. Snow crusts the lake edge. The sound of ash falls. The snow is ascending in concordance with words and the ritual of words. It is a language which sweetens the bristle and then slackens the Aleppo pine, it is this upward and downward tone, a lilt of wind through needles.

Victory is a sickness. A dangerous refuge is taken by touch. Your freedom is half faraway, is half impatient. No, you did not lose, through death, the body's first sharpness.

You were close to the city she fled. You slept in body armour as the shelling began.

‡

Attack at Fromelles, 1916

The bombardment was held off. There was no further target, and the last devil of the first fire was delayed. Everyone stopped, was held. It seems that time itself was detained, as if we froze in the ochre light. It seemed we were more and more jaundiced while images and receptors altered our absorption of time. The enemy saw us. They saw more and more blue through the gas. Our mood, under surveillance, under the region's aftermath, loosened. Discretionary, the light under the snow within the snow loosened, until the question of snow itself gave a looseness. There was a softening. The injured people softened. You among The Dead, didn't like the injured. You made no differentiation, though you were one of us. Some creatures, small of breath charred, destroyed, crawled in slow circles among the rubble. We too, creatures of air, darkened the snow. The region's looseness, appetite's aftermath, distorted. The particles of the enemy inhaled our particles, breathed burning hair, choked on our skin's vapor.

Now sleep among the injured, we say, shifted. They say the injured see more and more cobalt, a circadian leak, a left glow in opposition of colour. Leak by leak danger stalled between us. The untruth grew. Contaminated us. Visible lies drifted through the ruins. They were spies, they were neighbours.

There began a simple reality. We would no longer travel between the mileposts we made. They were going to leave. And like any other soldier, he fell in love with The Medic.

He was not a good man, this assassin, but the mythical world is full of his brand. Perhaps justice unfurls in the banner of time, some swelter of hell where sweat burns like acid. For now, mink's glands empty into the sweetest perfume. We preserve the inseparable odour between the wax seal and the film between the ambrosia's circuits. We smear the lines.

Fortified by the mute trees, his body burst and we rehearsed his eyes in an electric camouflage. A cloud line floats over a quick tide. Skin to skin, the water's surface spelled his name. Mare Anguis' crescent, a strange silence, pecked at the midday sky. When he looked up, his gaze, as if skyward, floated, but there was only a ceiling. It was always the same when the men's deaths came. Death came when they looked upward. And we, with faith lacking, pressed to our brow, like some angel's skull, Gabriel's thumb in consternation. Steam filled the room, like thick drips of dew in a limestone grotto. Grains of ice patterned the window. In the coming minutes, in the daytime shadow, he turned his back. He caught glimpses: sun under the trees where redbirds vanished in the brush. He wanted to belong to the candour, the blush we bore in faint memory before the edges swallowed him.

‡

Pozieres, 1916

With precision the barn closes its door to the wind and the Waler horses fade.

The plain's anatomy shifted. From a marked location: unexplained bombs. The horizon is a slender entrail streaked with winter light. It is mid-autumn. A soldier sobs in the trench as the tanks move past. Graven, his horse lay a mongrel heap at the top of the earth's fold. Her forelegs splintered. The sun fell the first day after the war began. Neither peace nor loneliness was buried beneath the earth.

She will wait in the dust, in the numb tide. She will dream of your soft hands holding a bunch of violets. Her pillowslip stings her cheek. She mouths the sharp syllables bathed in crisp white. She is a case study of a woman in a swarm of wasps; in her ears: a clicking, a serpent's tongue. The Dead's voices hiss.

Home was her memory of your hands—she took hold of your fingertips in shores against where water quivers. So to be clear, be clear. No signal. It is a flame enough, a sheen seen low upon mayday's horizon. Time as a seaweed mirror opens and sways as it sways, dips a double knot deep through kelp, rolls back buried wood flames. Maybe you never wanted to tell what the marred bodies claimed.

There is a moment the sea better tells of the hands you've held and held. You know it's not rational. Tide pools settled in trenches. Maybe now is when what she never wanted you to tell her, you tell her.

I love your quiet consciousness. I love you more deeply as one of The Dead.

You close your mind with so little persuasion. Pride's solace exists in this town where The Dead used to live, but the town must not be remembered, or if it's recalled, it must be rejected privately, viewed in patience, opened in night books of insomnia's thicket, alerted to dissolution at the cusp of dawn. Suppose the necessary images of you were memorised in urgency. For comfort, not for love.

You move north, you move east, you surrender to the dark. You walk forward into love as if meteors pit the boulevard, as if, in your concern for lack, you believed there were things that The Dead wanted you to surrender. The asphalt's patterns pave your way forward like abstract stepping stones under a streetlight's fluorescence. You glow around her shoulders as you walk by her side.

‡

The whole house broke into a wheeze. New algorithms marred the spaces between the bombings. An abyss opened as blackened pathways between each building like portals. She heard the people's voices in her mind's native tongue. A vessel that carried them over waters, beautiful in all its depth and resonant sounds, vibrations of their own survival. She always thought she would be calm facing abandonment. Now she knew who she was, an imprint decoded, a dabbling of supernatural questions, a daylight thief, her face in repetition disintegrated in the street crowds. She lacked identity. She pressed each animal horn to her teeth. She paused against gravity's dangers, the pleasure, her scandal.

The room was a lung, airless, yet still breathing.

An old rope swung on the little porch and the carriage leaned on the planking above the mud ruts. Without cages, a meddling brood gurgled in the yard of the sandstone house. The silhouette of peahens blurred the grass. You rode the wafer of light into the tunnel of images, your secret ruddy reflection over the white facade of the apple trees. There were no longer objects that required your attention.

‡

Messines Ridge, 1917

Confined to this tunnel with florescent lighting. Along the walls scored in calcite, she travelled. You escaped through the culvert where the river siphoned, and the tributary's conjoined voice dissolved. *If you are the ghost, you are not translucent*, she thought. She was calm in the face, but her pockets buzzed so feverishly that she thought to swallow handfuls of stones. Instead, she filled her pockets. Thus, her pockets swallowed the stones she collected beneath trickles of seawater. She found the end of the tunnel where the men waded into the water. She walked on, consumed, as she veered into the buzzing. She heard the sound, like a train charging up out of the sea's topography, but nothing lifted. Nothing lifted and she told you the roaring worried her.

The sea shapes itself when there is air lifting its surface. The winter mind. The courage of mud-evidence spread over her shins as she waded through dust. She felt the shape, the ventricle pressing up through the shore.

How many stones had she swallowed to maintain the measures between her body and the planet's density? The first thing she survived was a want she never asked for. Which meteor awoke her sense of self blame?

Your skin was sore when you walked through the alders. The skin of a ghost disappearing in angles.

You arrived slowly forward and would like to turn back.

‡

Mouquet Farm, 1916

In the trench, one kissed your forehead as they lowered you into the far end of the mound. They couldn't carry you up the hill though they tried. The Commander passed in a cloud of fire shell and radio frequencies. Only once did you see fear travel up The Brigadier's shoulders and flatten his eyes.

You were left with no instruction. No reconnaissance. Nothing was buried. Scent of chloride and lime spread against disease while carcasses were mauled by rats all through the camp.

You'd never been given permission to disclose the facts of your dissent. If asked, you would explore with impractical words, a loose entreaty.

You entered The Dead's house and waited. You stood against the quiet. The weeds at the window, a wild clumsiness. Before the soldiers arrived, you lay in the grass at night. You'd seen yourself in a tight horizon where streetlamp's triangular light floods a row of elm leaves. The trees, a conviction of spring, like sleeves of a woman's lace dress, a dream but once in this world—along with the ocean—and a few fruit trees, leathered by summer. Constellations cross an emptying shoreline; stars in linear regression weave toward you like a disordered border. Banks of the tributary are a secret path. The scent of bergamot is dabbed behind your ears.

She stands at the wardrobe touching your uniform, lint matching the shape of old conversations. Your voice, an air among the dreamless lenses. Epaulettes, a clover field, ribbons as a crooked drape of plane trees over your shoulders. Your language in rows, cultured as variegated wheat, is a stamp of arrangement. Lightly, you press your toes, like hooves, into soil. Moss grows over this shelter. There is a violet light, a softly shade, a tired sun, a solitude prayer makes of home. It streams through the crack under the door. It lifts through you. It dissipates. A scrawl in the ledger appears:

∴

I followed the long bookcase that led back down a hallway past the creek into the first cave, onward, where under a rock, in your father's country, I washed all your clothes before the battle. I motioned with my arms, my hands, under the nerves' pathways, under the supplications, I joined each thread in my fingertips. Your rifle balanced on that single point. I regarded this, regarded the Pacific spitting out its black oiled fingers, stretching its mixtures of hate through the lower sand bars. A distant algorithm which would bring you back. Yes, a line you'd follow, by all possible means, a voice, the ancestor of your body—a smile, a knee bone, each province of the aftertime. A small myth you concealed. It was a dangerous echo. And gentle.

∵

‡

She sees you in the heat, as the house closes in the gap between the louvers. The air burns. Motes drift past the mirror as you walk across the hallway. She gazes at the last image of the glass afternoon. The artillery supply wagon angles over the curve of the high cliff. Whole and still. She sees you. The eyes and mouth of the house close against the slanted sun. In the last light you see the militia-ghosts march. They lean into the heat and tread over the damp aftermath, spaces where the women's bodies lay. You will take with you the mutable undersound. Water fills the mind, fills the square stump where the schoolhouse stood: flat, swampy, thick with mosquitos. In the water weeds, you find the shape of their skulls.

‡

A horse stands in the room. He is cobalt, transparent, as if risen from a trapdoor. His ears are pricked. A confectionary snow scores his ribs and draws his outline. He listens to the afterworld. The room is a province. There is a look behind his eyes as he gazes upon the skylark's flightpath, as if he has long wandered against the city's wall, patiently stepping through thorn, until his outer body surrendered.

A loosening hand straps across his innocence. The honest strain of the body.

‡

The dark that shouldered the dark was not a human science. The ground beyond The Dead, beyond the troops, was a signal in which language ruptured, a loosening of the boundary. There was no ceremony now. And seven demons came to visit.

I saw you, and once thought you were real, they say.

The air clots your thin lips with confessions.

*I've got no one—*you say.

The telephone rings. There is a note on the rickety table. One pisser. One waste. One burial. Who were you.

Listen, you said.

I'll be here. I'll stay put.

At least until reconnaissance or serendipity appear.

The ledger continued:

∴

> *Until death can follow that breech between us, until autumn is translated and mid-air, in a room like this, an open skyline, in a twilight where the boundary of your voice is a departed memory, I'll long for you in the breaking. I'll hold the longing as a truth. I've stalled in the exact spot where the wheels jammed in the mud when the battle ended.*
>
> Magdalene's last note on the page—*They were hunting for me. I don't know how they knew I was here—*

∴

A holy darkness penetrates the room.

Slowly slowly you will use your resources.

You were not sure how to address this barrier, or who to tell. You would be foreign to this one account, the violence in the eyes of her longing. You lay now breathless among the reeds. She'd never seen what you'd seen, what The Dead had seen. Such as it is between you. As if you'd become belligerent and cruel, as if she'd been haunted by your worst side. As if you're supposed to be the enemy. A sensation of consciousness. The virtues you held faded out.

You and The Dead lived once as the same body. You became the effect of the energy, the open wound, and the undercut.

An old rope swings on the little porch and the carriage leans on the planking above the mud ruts in the yard. Without cages, a meddling brood gurgles in the dirt patch before the sandstone house. The silhouette of peahens blurs the grass. You ride the wafer of light, your ruddy reflection blushes the white façade of apple blossoms, as autumn fruits ripen early.

Death Speaks:

∇

Dead horses, shot one by one, were left in rows. I etched cinders into the dry lines where troops once tested their instincts. In sobriety I stop at every grove and speak to your ghost. Burr marks score the violets.

Across the range, across the many worlds laid in sediment, hate survived. The midday sun blushed the grass. Upwards, beyond the fires, seven rouge troops fell. Should they descend where the atmosphere answered, I might have understood their language, the ravine, the fold of rocks, the mitigation of creek dusk. Mathematical and far, they parted now: as soldiers, as objects of comparison, a gift, a wavelength, a reverberation. They told me I too must die in a small severance despite their courage.

It is said there were thousands who existed for years after death in this bright stream. A possible world without light. Amber scents of thyme drift past.

Every step I heard some distant bell. I heard it as a spiritual dare. I entered ethereal projections as if my own reflection were absorbed into a chamber. In the mute night, in my clumsy heat, I waded the shadow-lines beneath sapling hawthorns. I entered a small lake. It lay like a black pupil over the charred ground, a membrane, a thin eternity. Alien, in pre-existence to the fresh soil. And I, in my hour, sat in service to the misery attached to this place. It was not intolerable, but so then I am implicated.

In forgiveness, I'm hallowed out. In forgiveness: immeasurable.

Hallowed in, I am sovereign. The waters swayed me. I was no saviour. Across old battlelines, entangled electromagnetic fields, I follow dark mounds of granite, the earth's sutured skin, a nervous system, a spine trailing under Saturn's exodus.

Let me disassemble the danger. In my singularity, let me warn your ghost. Let me list clearly what happened.

But understand, there is more than one way to present it. If one suggests there is no state of perception, that perception itself is animate and whole, then there is no window of objectivity wherein, while speaking, I must illuminate a correlative gesture of uniformed imagination. It is all at once a sad dilemma.

I imagine the parched uneven pin oak leaf from the tree you planted. I imagine the nerves cut at the neck. The injury was read.

Tender your fingertips travel over my collarbone, under the brine, chokecherry-dry on my tongue. You climb the sea wall, the salt field; you were marked; you were without panic, solid in the wake of your weapon.

The infantry continued through the accident scene, a pack march beneath a shield wall. The sky, a carborundum sketch between centuries. Here, the ancients held the bridge in place; you were pinned above bush-marsh, funerary crimson undone on your lips, undone on my lips.

To mention the mind is to mention a derision. Incomplete, our relationship embodies my failure.

You held the gun. The gun held me. I was in love. I noticed things.

Let's say simply, it was a savage attachment.

Voices, consistent in their progression, in their movement toward change, hounded her up the gorge. She received, as she must, a certain shadow, a passion. *Were I a human*, he said. His murmur, prehistoric, urgent. War bells rang at noontime. She turned and looked down the hill. Bees mapped in a thrum. A guidance by which she was briefly consoled. Sweat stung her eye. Her hip tilted under the weight of the pack. Even if time is an illusion—more quickly, Camargue was a speck of dust far down the ravine. She'd passed through an ordinary cosmos that stretched above the mineral paths. Silica constellations shone through creek dust below. Salt, the taste of her labour, shattered under her feet as remnant snow.

The curve of a great being swept over and between her visions, a fleck in the canyon. Magdalene's sternum inhabits immaculate flames, mother to the mother of a medallion-sun. Madonna inhabited Madonna. *We were remedy to each other*, I thought. I thought again of the man's voice, it lifted as the sound of a body in a tide, in surrender, in a streak of shouts.

Δ

‡

Thistle Dump Armistice

You waited in Middlesex, ordered a Guinness at the Inn. Sea of crisis, south serpent. Lake of Perseverance, Lake of Death. You don't know how the moon entered this, but a thousand seas spilled as litany to quench your thirst. Mare Parvum, east of Inghirami, Incognitum, Novum. You study the map, your breath shrunk into a small sip. The Dead point to the map's torn edge just under the lamp. Above the mapping they stood naming the plateaus, the ravines, the wasted arrows.

They would follow you there if they could. The hum of wires placates the creaking wheels of a passing truck. The future surrendered into one soundless flush.

After you left the valley of Maria, after the eighth battle, you arrived at the west marsh, where the November snow fades the maple leaves, and a brick church abandons the cemetery's thistles. In High Wood at Longueval the memorial trees steady a square paddock.

Oak's driftwood branches flood the grass and their fossilized burls, like coral, strangle the gnarled tree trunks. You came to the commons, the perfect square, a grid where the brushfinch flatten in the rye. This providence began in dream. Nowhere in the district. No horizontal. No longitude. No radiant rays. Only copper crusts—crowns pressed into mildew uniforms lay across the furrows. The guardian birds would not return. No detailed sightings, no brambling, nor goldcrest, no cuckoo, no jackdaw. No officer to mourn the detachment of shell-torn wings. No singing in the valley reported. Each ghost warbling a cast of exodus. Somewhere in the silence you march back through the pasture. Your mud brown boots flatten stitchwort stars, and up the verge, a glint—a wet harvest. The houses there did not exist. The earth recedes. To know time is to observe this season. A nearness broken into a second waking.

The oiled clouds settled as a windbreak over afternoon paddocks, a cadmium bronze glows between woolly thistle and knapweed. Now, their bodies untroubled ash slips like spotted, pancreatic leaves beneath the ground. The gate opens into the fallow beyond the gentians and wild anemones. You enter a star's interior. A saffron-metal reflection burns your eyes, and in physical remembrance, the chiffchaff's *pip pip* ruffles the oldest sun, as a pressure beneath your skin. The trees went on talking. You moved through twilight's burial room. *Where did they touch you?* one of The Dead asks.

It was a feminine death, a spiral down your arm. The paratroopers landed in the she-oaks as Magdalene lay the letter on the table. As the soldiers lay him down you decided to go home. To leave without having. He was not meant for the small things, not meant for you who have gone now into the sheen. The imperial mass of an empire now lays a gallery upon this ridge.

The arrival of day birds in rhythmic streaks. Day birds clustered as a woodland froth.

They were slight namings, a reflection over the verge, a glint among the rye grass. You were stubborn in your silence.

There is a distant falling, a portrait of your face. The Dead held separate glances upon their shame. They recorded into the ledger:

.·.

To describe what happened we began with the worst experience. An entry point now the blank earth lays in paragraphs. We write through occlusions, acidic spills, cicada's pulse in my tongue. I am caught in the grass where agapanthus coppers in the sun.

.·.

Awake in opposite hues.

Cargo ships and steam rises and sways backward across the sea.

You see them stand in the snow which lays over the gulch in a topography of archipelagos and temporary dunes. You're intimate with the reversals of light as the dusk descends. The afterlife gleams. Is this translation or song. You've come as witness into the unknown beyond whiteness, unassured. There was an hour we stood in the doorway. As if at home in a language of a deeplight. You glimpse between the trees to see their shadows. They step through air. A whereabouts, a voluptuary pattern in language guides them. A strange narrator rests between them and the estuary sustains what is written. You consider my words luck. Then disagree.

You told them—*The big dogs never gave us the basic skills. Another digger taught me everything I learned. When they ask you for something, make yourself really dumb—*

Heat lowered through your sacrum. This was no theory. No trick of your mind to cease. Diamond patterns in the carpet tunnelled your pass-out point, a breath slowed in arrival to lift you away from his grip.

Did you not fell? The Dead were curious.

Years later the intelligentsia told you who he was as if to explain the why.

They found him in the barn, rope-hung from his left ankle, his face broadaxe spliced. You never gave your location. Calcite swung in the rope's shadow as you read the many omens: telluric currents, the soil broken in clamshell, a robin's terracotta plume. A radiance in their voices when they told you his skull silvered and shook from the scalping, a glow of coins scattered like ice over the lake beneath his head.

‡

After the battle at the Somme, a forest of stunted birch blanched the mountain. No human element remained. You drew our self-portraits across the terrain. You swept your hand, as guest, over the perimeter.

Your thumb pressed The Dead's eyes into still life, and you fingered the horizon's traces of iron.

They're buried now among the immortals. You marked the scene—

SCAPA FLOW

‡

At sea level the warship was a spectre. Luminous at one moment, eternity's termination the next. Magdalene saw its angles as a receding geometric on the vista, a white wake swallowing a towering polygon, a self-contained city surging along a waterline. From sea level she gauges the folds: salt plane's parallel shadows, the waves origami. A slow entity dissipates from her will, is released at various junctures—perhaps under duress, and begins to fade. Most likely in plot rooms, belly deep in the chambers, test-fires, calculated in symmetry with her breath, oceanic impulses, the air liberates from her lungs and brine placates her throat.

We're all likely murderous, you said.

An energy slips through her mind. You arrive the moment she looks down the horizon, as if looking through a rangefinder, and knows someone will not come back alive. You might cut and leave, you think. But for a while, what's normally, plainly said, must stay inside. What stays inside is an attention to movement. A secret word thrashes. No one will get to it. No one will hear it. Not even you, though it bangs its knuckles against your skull.

You said it would hit her, the shoreline, the waves sheen, but you no longer knew what was true. A cross-out Saturn, the waves, with their silvers and touchings. One is made by thoughts and then through her thoughts you knew. You couldn't carry the space between the body and the memory of the body. The earth swam with you as you swam among the shadows.

You think about the dream. You think about the ship off-course, bombed in the night. You think of the men when the sharks slipped through atramentous sub-waters. Once it happens, once you, in the sunless, vacuous waters, slip the wild tracing of another world, among the black tips and the mouthing, you will not be mistaken, you take your own happiness and declare it. It is a ghost language, the volley of the body over the ghost ocean. The narratives are your passion ascending. Mercenaries at nightfall, healed by language. The tongue asserts a mouth of silence in trepid English, what might expand, what might break union what might kneel among the waters. The silence a kind of listening.

The illusion of a sphere came to her, and with it, the splendour of repair which held within it a dark mineral, a carbon imprint. Her whole face turned slightly farther away. Her eyes followed the speed of the pallid boat as the moon slipped up from the ocean's swell; Mare Insularum, a numbing among the Sea of Nectar, Mare Nubium, clouds of vapor or of foam, an arrested consciousness, a soul within a soul, like waters within the waters, temperate, seeking peace, seeking solitude far from fear or dangers—

After the ship vanished, she wrote on the last page of the ledger:

∴

> *Row now my soldier after the smallest sun, after grief slips through your swollen wrists. The current breaks over you.*

∴

Once you and she were just two people walking into the clear night. You gaze into a dream of the street's end. You stood in the meadow.

You stood before the house where smoke softened the fence line. In her blouse you see her form in fire. This was her third death, where she drowned in fire's doorway. Your lungs witness fire's stratum. The house an anthem upon the crest of the iron-burnt harbor, a searchlight.

Even now she is gone, proven too late to speak. Her invisible country fills with signals.

You'd come to understand there would be no intercession. What acolytes remained were now orphaned.

You remember the veteran grass in which she lay, looking upward to Saturn's sputtering rings.

Accession Number, Unassigned

Archived in a metal box, you nest among old military certificates, dental charts, French language enclosures, and your mother's plaintive letters. Readied, the earth horses saddled and tested, you travel light's blaze off a Trakehner's forehead. The river's sedge outspreads Eridanus' chart between Achernar and Azha as you flee the murder space.

Your mother presses ancestral bloom into the pillow-slip's cotton, says she hasn't prepared your burial soil. Moonlight impales snow under elm's dappled canopy. Your horse brays, innocent under the ease of the stuffed air that presses your skull, and presses bindweed flecked by sunlight, the bearings of follicle and grass—she soaks the black scalp of the meadow as if to abide love.

Fascinus fosters a belief in war—ancestors, lynched by your own hand. Their teeth spread over fields of this little dark you stitch, and so you are stitched, into smallness.

There is one memory in which your one life was lost in the saving. It was the first vanish season, and the men descended upstream to merge at the cramping bell where the river-current's slow examination spurns salt to ice. An oceanic sweep where the earth turns her back, a celestial death, tectonic breath shifts beneath the earth.

An amber trickle of saliva unthreads your lip, silverfish sluice birch roots, and a cobalt halo streams your left ventricle.

This is how you become your mother's unbearable ear, her pleas in everyday speak. Soaked in incalculable elements of blue dust and military gravel, the pun for the seer's eye measures suspicion's construction. These dispatches of the one who was long loved in celebration.

Helmet blown, scent of asphalt in humid air. A palm size fragment of cranium the colour of quartz. This gunmetal archive glows. By accident, she hears you. You say—*I am not yet star. Not yet previous.*

I might wait for time to pass and find my way back to you.

As only I, in you, alone slept beneath the heath.

Above my unmarked grave the night sky's ochre bruise rusts. A sack of mist left where the bodies' goodness sleeps, sullied in dawn's grasses.

O haunted mouth, O my haunted mother.

Your body comes to finish its work.

The black river prepares for a boat to cross: The Dead's entry point. Geometries float from your breast, obtuse angles and isosceles. Dead relatives arrive and sit on your bed. They stand in the door, drink coffee, bullets drift through their mouths. You are asking if your mother is there, if the whole encroachment of the sea lies against you. A procession of ancestors call across the sharp depth of the frozen field; laughing or burning, their torches draw toward. There is a small dream sound in their voices. Leave, in what name, and how, as your feet enter a clear current. In death's grey sacrifice, there is no sparing of knives slipped into each other's ribcage, nor a garrote's narrowing over the throat in a lost breath. The wind picks up a doe's scent. They toss their weapons into the Mazurian marsh and leave burial masks on the porch of your distant house. The swarm of their cast hands is gently given. Then they pause to

carve a crucifix from elk horn. Now it's your brow they anoint
by morning.

WORLD WAR II

‡

In the room of her lover, she never looked back.

There is no courtship with a lover, there is only a door that shuts the morning away. *I am yours into the unknown*—the body says. The virtue is sweet, but you don't collect it. The black sea, the black liquid of a black room, a black tea—every tactical instinct is biological, punctuated in the dark. All the blackening stilled. As if descending. It is black against the wall where a milky blossom of quartz light spills over the rug like a cut-out in the shape of her dress. There is a thin ring finger materializing. An ionized glow covers the hollow curves of her collarbone as she shifts under the reading lamp. Her silhouette, asleep in pieces, burns topaz. A rose fades on the bedside table. A new galaxy leeches beneath her. Only her heat heavies the room.

Awake and alone, the white scent of grass washes through the curtains. She tastes scarlet, a humidity off the Pacific. Clamminess wefts the room. A book lays open on her chest. A book lays open, and a sign lifts from the book—a scrawl of light, a mosaic, little mealy figures, smears on the horizon, longitudinal traces—glints of mica, carbon bubbles. No answers. Little wisps of people. These transparencies remain undiscovered. Not characters. Not things. Not even ideas. Under this materiality she surrenders in secret. What really matters to her in what is recorded—an elemental force, a vibration of that thin line between the silt and the space where spiders gather in the pine trees surrounding the house. She wonders—*Why weren't the inhabitants tagged in the book? The pages marked…?*

This happens in the quiet. A flame, as her image vibrates—she leans into the remedy of feeling. Her tribe's gathering is still there—the nothingness floating between and above her. It continues to spread. She watches it. A stain on the ceiling expands large as a continent. It wasn't easy to extract. You are among the blotted out, the blotted in. You went without pride because she knew you wouldn't come back. She lay, looking up at the ceiling, a veil torn open to light, a meddling space, indistinct, gleaming as if splashing upon the surface of a wave. A watery, inhuman anchorage, a double image: she saw herself as if in a small boat drifting out. *We never called it a border, but that's what it is now, between you and me—we, as fundamental "others," an opposition binds us. I am the thing you see less or more for the way you see me. You are the means of seeing by which I see you.* She'd like to think you and she were the same person. *Your face upon my face, your gaze in repletion.* This is to say you hope her belief is something true. You believe in the fossils flattened in the pools, lakes, water-filled ditches. You believe that into your old life you brought all your old habits, the people you conquered, your collections: kimonos, bone helmets, trade beads.

She forgives the widow maker trees before they drop over the small dog rushing beneath smears of ash. The courtyard filled with weight as if a boundary between mediums were absorbed by the crabgrass and thorn. *Yea, I want to be going,* you say. To sit beneath the regrowth under the waves of the black kites—a vector traps whistling preludes as they drop burning branches from their beaks, sip by sip, to flush out field mice and lizards.

…a dream sequence…

In the first dream, you came to her the night after it happened. When you say it happened, it was less than an accident. After the accident, at the beginning, your eyes closed with each exhalation. She wanted you to choose what exists, to imbue what is just. She took clarity in this belief. She asked about your country. It was slow. She waited to see if you'd move. Your injury was reviewed. It was quiet. She turned her back. Signs faded. Restrictions grew. *My country, where I was, it didn't exist.*

You weren't hopeful to find new beliefs from within this dimension. You are old and filled with patience. At best you'd be staying a while, within the field's edge, to meet others as they crossed.

That night you wrote on a napkin: —*It's not a disease that makes us exist in two dimensions*—

You met her at a grey station house along the trainline. A soldier and a seer—your long conversations held silence. Your habits became her habits. Under the wilding you hoped the enemy might be depleted. But no such luxury came. She travelled with you and wondered how to measure the danger.

Your hand rested on her lower back as you guided her through the streets to the town's edge. There were no more screenings at the border. She knew she was the only person seen. An ironic existence, to live in the silence of this warning. To live within a warning which is the silence of a ghost. You, The Dead, the warning. Another person met by wrongdoing, a star brighter by distance. She sat too close, shoulders locked a stream of light between the two of you—serried filaments pressured the space, invisible cords, tender stems, reaper vines, taboo bindings. You distanced yourself for a moment, affirming the vague undercurrent, but a slow physical integration opened between your lung's exhalation which was her exhalation.

There was no immediate attraction, but there was an archway of white apple blossoms, and a dark road beneath. She'd travel the furrows deepening under your eyes, your cold refulgence, her expression, an implacable current; there wasn't an end to the landscape. Your eyes swayed as if a current of water under minnows, like a sheath of broken mirrors. Reeds skimmed the surface, and sometimes she could see through this dark.

She lived with the signs—the signs of displacement. She lived with the trouble of guilt like living with the trouble of drowning, a phobia for undertows, a faint obsession of drifting too far from shore. It was also the trouble of evasion— what she forced herself not to consider. Sitting beside you she sensed an insecure series of gestures. You scratched your forearm's scar where the knife sliced just above the wrist. She noted a twitch in your upper lip yesterday when she waited in the food line.

Two men arrived to resolve her nightmares; they handed her a splitting maul and star-picket. The splitters advised the common ways to glance at an object with an axe. They warn you of the danger if you miss a blow. Half upright, the blade might catch the nervous system of a barn swallow, and in full lift, snare a nest. But this was a kind of terrestrial impalement only visible in certain latitudes.

You were taught to restructure each dream with completion.

That night she woke, she was talking to you. But in fact, she was talking to a soldier during combat, warning him of a sniper ahead.

You didn't know him, but you think you may have met him once.

You stared into the end of the pickaxe, stared into the injury on the other side of the ledger.

The ledger, like tickertape, continued:

∴

I steal myself. I mark myself. I am pacified by guilt. I'd said no, but already, I'd say yes.

I can't do what you do. What do you do. You make the wrong thing difficult and the right thing easy. You'd been cared for. What we said in the past. It was over, the potential for kindness in death, the target, the temptation to meddle in a musculature, a disease among the elements. For the purpose of what I have said, each form of truth makes no difference to the question. I am asked if I can hear and make no response.

∴

She lifted herself and sat up in the dark. It might kill her, the world, or it might remove her bravery. She crossed the bedroom toward the stuffed chair that was centred against the wall near the only window. The room was airless. She sat in the chair and looked out the closed window. She saw the trees shift in the wind.

A sea washed over her. It was a language she couldn't contain. A blackout wave, a voice trickling through a small incision. A darkness leaked into the open room. You stirred in this darkness on this summer night. You stirred the dark like ash. Her body burned. You were one of The Dead who would not wait. You didn't understand. You were of ordinary worth but couldn't contain your need. You'd tracked her for months.

You were still in her mind. This energy. You were an energy. A physical strain drew you. To name the pain is to name the small acts of possession. You ran your finger down her sternum in the dark. It was a sexual wounding. The repetitions removed themselves, the wounds within the wounds, like words becoming rhythmic.

Already the night inside the waves shifted. The Guards appeared, shot between the train cars, a small unpredictable militia. The longest week of the year had happened, had happened: the longest exchange of fire during battle.

There was a cue. Looking out to the lawn made her dizzy.

Impassable fires on the hilltops, wild and distant. Black thistle, damp ash, and smoke penetrated the soldier's skin. The wounded and The Dead, held to the edge of the hill. It's always The Dead who end the battle. And it was always The Dead who found the narrow canyon. The canyon opened to a lake where a mulberry tree stood like a warning finger. The ranks broke and slipped away from the hostiles. Lame now, the horses arrived late, though had left early. She looked at the high sun and knew exactly how their death would begin. A tipping of light over the dry grass, she knew not to state the dead one's name.

You don't nearly die, you die, she thought.

You come to the window. Survival was a trial, luck over strength, even for the least weary. The sea was careful with the horsemen, but also unscrupulous. Anyone could say tenderness came with the intensity of death. You didn't know you were to stay, and you left them on the plane. You fled, inhuman, but you still held your pride.

You couldn't understand why you broke in two, nor what travelled with you.

She lingered in the repetitive thought of what you had told her: *They are testing me. If I die by my own hand, I lose. They're trying to make me suffer.*

It was out of proportion, a bucket sloshing between her temples that wouldn't still.

‡

When Magdalene sat at the desk you also came to sit at the desk. Your flesh had been remade from the mangrove's sediment. She wrote, *I was conscious of the dangers. I was conscious of the swamp.* Given the narrative, she considered the premonition and then its opposite as a maneuverer. You allowed yourself into the easement. You'd leverage the abyss as structure. It was not easy to extract.

She never believed the impunitive nature was your nature. *When you embrace impunity*—she wrote—*contempt sets in.*

∴

—*With you, my unreliable stranger, my strange alliance, I knew then I was well into wilderness*

∴

She once directed you: *Draw a horizontal line; draw a vertical; draw a line that speaks to the other line you just drew; draw a weak line.*

You drew a line. You drew the far darkness of the house that drew a soft line around its sleepers; there is no collision within the haze of their dreams; they do not traverse in any direction.

You draw a line between body and self. In this way, you can admit that the physical damage is real, you can acknowledge that you are both hurt and hurting. In this way, she can also look at you. As she remembered, she remembered his hand darkening, the touch, the sound of graphite. She writes into the ledger:

∴

No, think again ghost, something sweeter, a gateway at the edge of the aquifer. I know where you live, my little ravening, a dark speck in the imagination. You left no short passage through my grief.

∴

If she could be as direct and simple as possible, she would tell you what she understood, but the catching was fragmented, only a series of hazed vignettes to be avoided. Avoided, yet they persisted like contractions. She couldn't make a story where there was none. What she could tell you is there was never a map. A travelling through trauma, through time, through locations given only through blurred snapshots. She wasn't sure what you were after. For those travellers lost at the border, between banks of rubble in the realm of the unreckoned, logistics were lost. The location was only a template. You rode the edge of the wave on a prow.

The spirit waters clot, and the sea fills your lungs. Yes, you have an Alsatian and a river to cross. So, you finish, you've stayed long enough. You are ending and promising no end.

‡

You said it would hit her, the weapon of the mind, with a slowing of breath. She put herself in this position. She held all the weapons she needed to win. She lived in a paradox of her consciousness. Her values, etched plainly by each of her visions, contradicted her desire for peace. Often, she'd been disillusioned by intimacy. As if horns locked around her heart. When she examined her thoughts, she glimpsed, on occasion, that she lived under an oppressor. What mattered, she concluded, was to keep her empathy alert.

When she left the train, she wandered the tracks and found a clearing. She stood in the Eastertide's woodland. Spring's absence that year was noted in the snow's traces over wheel ruts. It was the second coming of winter, the morning fog like smoke shimmered and flattened beneath her. Gray masses of pear trees scored the skyline, blossomed like the coiffures of old women huddled over a bridge game. The ravine, drawn ragged up through the undergrowth, remained charred, but less spindled, less poorly defined from decades past.

The trees uprooted along the storm banks; sable branches of orchard trees felled in a chevron pattern along the river's bend. The enemy scorched the barns, but left the cattle to wander, dehydrated and starving.

‡

If I draw attention to it, you might think I was guilty somehow. No good would come if I told. She recorded this in the ledger.

The rank structure was not arbitrary. We understood the taskings, and we'd undermined the command's authority. At the access point, we assembled the kill chain, dispelled our suppression. Their horses, spooked, hit the barbed wire.

The runnels down the cinderblock wall spelled doom. *I am leaving the empire or should I say it left me.*

Let me tell you, there was no time left. —he said.

But she couldn't describe the heat within and between her hands, the palm lines, the layered bridges. The crescent pattern on her palm—a swirl of Mare Ingenii measures the space between her fingertips by inches, and mimics tiny layers of earth embedded in her fingernails as evidence of rape. With war-crimes the recurrent signs are buried by human pacts.

Years later, an old woman read her tea leaves—a garland of cracks in the cup, a blaze of weeds shaded each battle. She says nothing as she sees.

I came to tell you about my crimes, you said. But they did not hear you.

Too soon your energy burns away. Stars, your carriage, give entrance to strange greenery, the world's new weathers.

Without jeopardy, without the new sun, without the path along the river's slipway, your enemy's gaze, hushed the horses among chokecherry. Her curse mildews in the teacup. Cyanide ampoules sit on Magdalene's bedside table.

You aided the enemy by cumulative harm, sedimentary breath deepening each atmosphere, and now cameras are trained to her backyard.

Homeless in grief's home; the earth's unbridled grasses traced your wandering.

She followed you through the landscape's lingual gesture.

And called you in her mind to wake you—

Oblivion. Did she cause or crave it. The odds were not clear. She was drawn back to the hectares where the men disappeared. Grassfires surrounded the faces of the missing. If she'd seen your face, it wasn't your true face. No one knew you were here in your death. There remained a kind of ringing between the two of you. You needed to terminate the sound. There was no honour in the toll. She said—*don't ask me who you are now*. Your physicality is two-pronged. Among The Dead you'd died yet didn't. There are always patterns among brave ones. Gross continental drifts are processed by physics: seafloor undulations, garnet folded in common rock. Your wound wouldn't be medicated beside the woods, beside the marsh, nor in a strangle of grasses.

It wasn't long ago she'd given up all the safety of her possessions. She had no need of the protections of heirloom lockets, teacups, drawings, or her mother's memorial portrait, but she remembered the epitaph: *I am your shelter, I did not die, but dwell in your sleep,* and she could sketch her coat of arms. The year she was born all her ancestors ceded. They didn't fight longest but fought first. There was no past. No language. No record. Thus, a certain labour amplified upon her, the labour of transition as fractal patterns faded. Armorial brass rubbings carried off in weed-torn grass decayed alongside her forebears' tombs. *Honor Virtutis Praemium.*[1] She used to polish the escutcheon quarterings filled with oak trees, lions,

[1] *Honor is Virtue's Reward*

banners, and cryptic symbols. Designed over centuries, the patterns tarnished as if rubbing sand between her forefinger and thumb.

Your dog tags hid beneath a floorboard in her bedroom.

As you were, in answer, she prepared to sleep her last sleep.

When you stopped at the soldier's church the font bowls froze into crusted waters, the chapel room was dark. You felt a single consciousness. You felt an ablution in your throat as if you'd swallowed the enemy's blood—but there was no likeness in your captors. The murder came when you were ill with apology.

No one can explain the medical experiments: a small boy, strapped to a chair. At intervals his head receives a hammer blow. At intervals you tried not to produce the vision. At intervals throughout the prairies, warriors slow cooked their enemies. If you know yourself, you must know your enemy as equal. It's the only means to transcend each battle. All you know is that sadists move with transparency through each century. The only points at which she could bring you back were the gaps between the infinite where the infinite was recorded.

The ghostly gods lay among the powdered purple mysteries of fluttering clematis vines; the moment the air shifts upon the skin, upon the motherless sea, upon the seams of a thousand faces.

You lay your body down at the tributary's beginning which expanded like fingerlings toward the landscape. The mistle thrush, pipets, and redstarts disappeared beyond the shell-torn mud. You heard the fusion of your voice among the hum as the tanks retracted.

With the arms of your invention, someone who lives at the estuary among the sage and cedar knows the work was without amends. The work was not over. You are among The Dead, and The Dead did not declare your lives. Your bread lay intact upon the table as the inquisitors crossed the field toward the farmhouse. You capitulated your prayers and proceeded with the shooting. The same prayers by which they now turn your body over. But your body is dispossessed. Soulless, weightless, your anatomy thins out. Your gaze is a radio wave, small concordances, the scent of your pipe tobacco when walking on the lane after a fresh rain.

Death sat with her in the dark. *Mercifully*—she thought—*how beautiful it is.* Dawn after the darkness, like a swan at the window. The rising sun. The sky quieting. Strange, the sound she felt speaking within her when she was alone. Her eyes were wide open, she looked once more on the sun, a red rose on which she feasted. She lay still within her own seeing. *It is plain*—she said—*It's my hour.*

Saints whispered through the wallpaper. There it was in her body. A great fire. As if her body was thrown from the boxcar. As if she skidded off the tracks leaving her identity behind. A dying time. *Who am I in damage. What have I done.*

She regarded her complications. The complications of morning. She never experienced the pressure, the mosquito besieged night, but she remembered your admission. It kept her awake as she lay. Unfolding, her voice opening into nothingness a stream or a province in a night which drifts like rays from the sun of another galaxy. Her boat set down upon the venture, a shoreline somewhere and now younger than she was now, the people she knew, an articulate people who died for their belief in this plane so that her body might traverse its margin.

‡

In the afterworld, time accelerates. At the last battlement she met the workmanship of ghosts. Ghosts of many levels, their ghost-myth—sybaritic and luminary. They wandered across the grassy plateau at Whitsun. She didn't follow your death. She followed the dreams in which you spoke—the ghost voices into ghost voice—it was air, it was ghost dream and water. Your ghost met her at the gate, and it was the dream speaking ghost in a ghost dream.

Voices, they run, they are a cause and a workmanship. Ghost inside the ghost, you swam the sun divided by water, you knelt at the church. You couldn't call for their help as you remained in this other world, an observer through blackthorn winter, dogwood winter, this season of grass. This season, earth, like the old command, never believed in surrender. The grass, dry underfoot, the waves like arches which drown her lover, as she dove for the communion. In this Teutonic valley she lay among the voices, immovable—burnt orange, basaltic taste on the tongue—a blood ash, and the waters of Mare Serenitatis.

‡

Ravensbrück, 1942

Salt swept the earth. Eyeless, into the infinite, the prisoners stood in line against the long lengths of wire, against a boundless fence, as their hope stretched a warped threshold.

The field roots bent upward from the under dust. Punishment came to the soldiers as a slow restoration, cracks of blood on their lips, heat quickly marked their foreheads, salted-crowns bloomed beneath their helmets. The soldiers sanctified the air. It was a clean reverberation—under vests, under pulse, under skull. They travelled the horizon. You watched them enter the gate; you recognized the question, masterful: love's restless view. You knew. The cause. The effect. You knew not to hold too tightly. Sentimental, you became what came toward you. You came to grief before the others. You remembered the young girls as they'd been at the village. The injuries became existential. The old forest's patterns of light stung. That night The Partisans left the village and gathered in the reeds. When the troops approached, a heavy unspoken blow, the group's silence weighed upon the sound of sobbing. She pressed a bloodletting, clamped her palm over her sister's mouth, pulled her small bones deep into the murk. You remembered the sun. A worn-out desire. You felt her emerge from the centre of the bullrush. If you held doubt, you held it in your heart: strange lotus, sugared with snow.

They cuffed the women to the rear, lowered them into a stress position. Only one woman, pregnant, stood upright.

‡

Darwin, 1941

Magdalene met you in the shelter room, the bunker below the electric substation. Water dripped in the corner and spores collected over your eyelashes. The room's exhalation was the scent of rust. A stranger, you were a neutrality, a deserter.

She measured your kindness against two rocks she kept in her pocket: one a weapon of protection, the other a catchment for prayers to St Jude. *Panic, an enemy's munition* The Dead told her.

You sleep close to the floor and so perhaps an insect crawls across the muscular wounds of your broad face. You imagine the room submerged in stormwater. Bluegill drift under the curve of your ribs like charms. You disappear into shaded surfaces; trevally gills and fins brush your collarbone. Having no one, you belong to water's terror, a depth taken by tide—a convergence wherein sea rips marrow from wave.

Upstream, a pelican's carcass floats in flood waters and trout bloated belly-up by the thousands.

You hear voices to the east pale against the bunkhouse echoes. The Doctor explained that search boats would not find the children's bodies for days as bones hit the river basin first before surfacing upward with the tide's surge.

The outer body is woven into the muddied bricks of the harbor. Within the limits of possibility there are gross achievements and a sense of efficacy. This was not the dream you were seeking, but in ways of seeking you witness what's given when you are found. When you are wound, you're omniscient. But are you quick or fatal?

Her body was found after the downpour along the Ota river. She lay as a small cosmology among the star's decapitated orbit.

Suppose the images were better without the direction of memory's language. The Dead were taken, tenable by translation, fingering all the scars where hate might be placed.

Something of the rain as a nerve upon the hour. Water's new pelt, the city as escarpment, nothing left to clean.

For the truth of love, not comfort, The Dead reminded.

In much of a muchness, it wasn't all one-sided.

Today Yesterday My Afterdeath

‡

You never knew what you wanted, what made you weary.

What you loved, the soldiers were not known to love.

You were not among The Dead's answers. You were alone and expendable, but you were with them.

There was a rationing of food and clothes, and suddenly no petrol for private vehicles. You always carried a fisherman's stool so you could sit somewhere in the shade and drink a flask of tea to disguise your dissonance. It was unlikely you could start a riot. It was unlikely anyone would think you were suspicious.

You worked as a guard at a date orchard. You saw things influenced under great force—the burning bodies flung into vegetation went shapeless.

And you knew the people would never be informed. Laws took care of the denizens' blindness, pressing a fast chaos through the decades. Trust is not trust. But still you insisted. *Believe me, they would not kill the criminals,* you said. You tried to impart yourself with an oath of forgiveness. Some stupid legacy within a legacy.

They died there beyond the shooting plane. A space of belief where a carpet of civilized citizens spread over the mud. The ally's truth, now a snow-slurred portrait. Your voice rose into a mercurial knot within The Dead's ears, roil of three-thousand dust-motes, a gun dark kill.

You thought you might be filled with compassion, not humility.

You walk toward a column of alders and dwarf plum trees.

The river borders the chapel which is only an abandoned clearance of pine and snakewood.

How often your grief repeated. How did it happen to ask for someone? You would never be alone now that you'd known them. Sometimes they touched you. Moments when their language drifted to the mid-fold. You saw their diminishment arrive. Your faith paused.

It was noon when it happened. You wouldn't come out, though they waited. They misunderstood the exit point where your apparition, as an answer, might come. In theory you were always shades. Certain obsessions congealed. What would it mean to see your form? A random smudge on your apartment door felt like an accomplishment. A fingerprint, the means of your grip. The Dead held hope for betrayal— that in this life you may still abide, but you tried to hold your mind toward the opposite. Leaves shudder between lanes of ragweed and goldenrod, a passageway a backward mirror … When you stood in front of the medicine cabinet I could leave your reflection, step into your form, finger your jawline as you shaved. Maybe too, you must think of another face within your face, or see within the glass the fields. They slept by lakeside reeds.

Though you could think of other possibilities in your marriage that led where you were, it sometimes happens that people participate in transforming a boundary within themselves and play against one another without awareness. Then we are allowed within ourselves a suppleness. You called this an internal transcendence, though in truth it may be a form of dissociation. Or an imprint in your DNA. Some people believe memories are genetically transmitted. Consequently, what survives may be a mix of beauty and subversive brutality.

You have loved who you do not know.

You have loved who you would not see.

You have loved who you could not see and read their translations on the walls in the old corridors between houses.

Different dialects occurred within the repetitions.

Your interior words, a linen remnant—stars and atoms and scholarship, a force told, a heat's firmament. The witnesses finished when the frequency opened.

You were a specimen that lived one week. Love's tactic was your only control.

The passing men didn't grieve. They passed through the tunnel as their unfixed world lifted their footprints off the field, blessed by nothing.

Yet once, in afterdeath, their eyes met a sweetness.

You have missed the wildest of them and the dull boil by which they sat in the fire. In long communion, the taste of bread, hollow in the caves of sleep, among the lantern wicks, their smoke smudged lips, from which silence hung a strange unsteady beauty.

Had they escaped alone you would have said nothing.

For the piousness of their wounds, you stabbed them with your fist and mocked their rank.

They let each other break in the pity of battle.

They were speaking as human. In your human speech.

At the hairpin curve, the attractive men disappeared into strangers. The street and the café's glazed tables survived the imagination, thumbprint dumb under terror's mid-air outburst. You were sloppy and so his belt tore you open. You cleaned the cup for The Orphan's milk. The body's tension invented fever

O, my little friend—they said—it is more about the *content* of being, what is held away from us in protection.

When The Scholar explained that the stream separated the town, like a bomb, the marsh heaved in the deluge.

Fire gutted the coastal trough, deepened the sky's grizzle. You were bleached in soot. You say The Dead were a blessing, your mother's laughter, an open door in a rainstorm.

Through the white horses they glimpsed kelp's betrayal of surf—stretching forward against foam into aspic. Firmament in premonition as if stilled in museum glass. Her hair, aglow in a bouquet of chlorophyll, sea-willows.

Say we were a blessing. Your mother's laughter, an open door in a rainstorm.

You and yours waited in the kill box.

You had requited the role of your ancestors.

That night your guardian was arrogance and plea: the self-obsessed always wield power. Eventually. Delayed resources retrieved The Orphan. You sensed her exposure, her ribs, a shored nautilus. Her head was shaved.

Because her family died in a car crash, she'd never look away from that country of sleep—buildings above ground, skies below. Through an outer door, she watched the corridor's edge, a hubcap's gleam, a town trapped beneath earth's crust. An exchange of places. She heard noon rush in the town centre, air sucking upward. You told her not to keep you here anymore. You couldn't do it. What you really told her was to follow.

There are certain points in illness at which the body turns against itself.

She understood the allies held a natural sense of rage over the necessity of basic justice.

The Dutch resistance, in advance warning, saved over seven-thousand refugees by sending people off in small boats to Swedish shores. The unwanted squadrons failed.

Is there a national characteristic of the enemy, which human survival waxes, wanes, plays victor—?

Of the men, she only liked the ones who would document their pain so she might hunt for the tools to heal them. At the feast she presented her winnowing basket embellished in seed-beads, pipes, the algal wing of a gull, the tiny book inked in gallnut and wax, the seven prayer sticks.

Maps divided the asters. Her witchcraft leads you to the corral where a colt carries you to the infinite.

To procure a medicinal solution, she read the remedy from the battery hen's scratches—insect-grit among barley. She understood that in the plagues of that one century curses outweighed scars, scars outweighed charms. By afternoon the hen house splintered into a deck of cards.

‡

Under the moon's mortality you listen to the cruel untired shore. You've defined the artillery, your preferences, your command. You've given this one star. Your resonant rejection, a lowering: rejection is spring's incubated arrangement, a structure, a sequence of preconditions. What you want to say, you don't. Every few seconds, somebody with or without an ID card on their neck disturbs you. The beaches here are ungroomed. The trailer park's washrooms are average, but there is plenty of hot water for everyone. You believed you needed to share where you were in order to gain repose and seek renewal. This is the language of a story which requires location. Who was the girl. Where were you that morning.

Her personal apocalypse is this page, after she turns her back, a breeze in the moment—her face, a stillness you can touch through the haze. In an incubated arrangement you ordered the pictures of the sun into a sequence of right to left. She wasn't anyone you knew. She is a cosmos.

The sea is like a disease breaking between two landscapes. She is tethered. Her body waits for a cure.

He wanted to be true. He wanted to be with you when night fell.

He told you not to keep him here anymore. Said he couldn't do it. What he really told you was to follow. He told you his identity was gone but you were not abandoned. He told you he would not travel through that last valley despite wandering through this other earth.

In lawful order, or in soldier's courage, courier pigeons swooped among cannon: disguised as hawk, disguising the horror. They were twins, and human by birth. One died. One didn't.

You repeated the phrases: the sapwood, the twining of bodies. They were physical. They were astral.

They both came in one uniform, tagged one shape, one size, under the wind whipped-radar, suits strategized across maps marched as foetal cells inside foetal cells, boot prints as exoskeleton tramped uphill behind them.

They were citizens who mourned the old languages—Latin, Aramaic, the rain's swift sound—miles past winter moss, heart's thumping in iron shields, hidden in boulders, and pre-fire pine—the human wound, disturbed by a dark brewing, the flame's shout, the zero level of a trooper's scream.

As the hooves of the cavalry's horses gained altitude, the sea's phrases sang in echo to the shoreline woods, washing the dividing line of boats outward toward the village houses.

Each prayer dated, each spectre catalogued, each dog-tag marked surrender stilled in the clumsy soil—

Remember on the eastern edge the troops retracted into hives of amaranth-weed and rubble. Remember even in effigy you were holy.

Today, Yesterday, Hereafter My Death

Death Speaks:

▽

I swallow the rotted air, Illyrian communion under the tongue. I spit as the ships charted toward equinox. Already smashed to the rubble of shoreline fish traps, Magdalene deepens the horizon's dark matter. As always, she was an extreme condition of mathematics.

The night I tried to stay alive I created a sequence of illusions.

I cannot quantify her affection for skinned rabbit stewed in dandelion petals, baked pear and eelgrass cakes, midsummer bundles of hyssop and rue tangled in her hair. Her consecrated feast spread upon the table opened our line of perspective.

Her letters of procession were recorded before the years of headstones and inscriptions.

There was no corollary between the horizon where we bathed our hands in saline, watched the swath of seagulls dive past our glasses of dry gin and spider's harvest of a new language inside the lake's scaffold.

We left our tonics on the terrace.

A city of sparrows descended the foreshore, a visitation less valuable than many, as the maritime gendarmerie patrol boats stalled in the strait's false coordinates where the sailors witnessed her small cottage. The hallway mirrors reflected a glide of pocket watches into wool, mud crusted knives, a small raven's shelter.

Uphill, we knelt in the haystack where her open vocabulary of desire was a partial crime. We were not done, but all the guns were fingers pointing from the doubts of strangers.

She furthered the blackout when she stepped into the periscope. Even then I could not touch her body or prompt a revolution. The stars were simply roadkill we could not perceive yet, a massacre map.

She and I were often lovers, unless one of us was dead, and so implicated.

She disappeared far into the trees not to become my wife, but to witness this conscience.

In daylight's tributary, confinement met her and the machineries of their baptized sun met her. Men among the machines met her.

Before they dragged her to the shed and doused the clapboard walls in kerosene, the men beat her. A skein of red-naped ibis wedged between her diaphragm and sternum and choked her. Their black beaks in flip-turns braced cartilage, a wishbone's ebb in her breath. The stars of the northern cross levelled her torso as her knees girded between Sadr and Gienah and a mineral heat bound her inner thigh. Upward burnished waters, the myth of flies in a gospel of vetch. A skeletal corridor of elm branches and a loosening twine of ropes snapped the wind.

I remembered all.

She'd been in a sitting position with her hands on her knees.

Drones tilted her jaw. The musk of a doe's neck blossomed when the room exploded.

Δ

‡

When you found Magdalene you were a non-commissioned officer overseeing a small group of men. Every boundary betrayed her. Was it your absence directly in front of her? The children were murdered, and the soldier thought this a beautiful thing, the death that was chosen, after hours of practice, no penance. The soldier's kill as beauty. This beauty was a soldier's work.

You wondered about her death. You wondered if your reaching for the momentary passage might give the dying relief. You wondered about your death. You were a bleak consciousness, scattered and lost. You were death and only the dying might see you.

From the assault platform nothing changes. At a regimental level, indemnity sustained the process. You want to tell The Dead softly. You want to go back further. You want to explain how the trajectory ends without counterbalance. The soldier did not kill a person. He murdered an idea.

But at the moment, you are among the north river's shared ablutions, a sway of water, the scent of wild thyme and clumps of blue grass high in the fields and on shore. You think of Napoleon's plane trees the soldiers planted. The oak the soldier's father planted in the yard when he was born. It is gone for certain. As is the house. Complicit in the ravage, even the camera light fails. You don't see the civilians burying the dead cavalry horses after the battle. You see reflection.

It wasn't a job, your life was his life, this kill.

It was a simple answer. The four children watched their father fall to the dust.

The horse's burial tombs were vetted by the old trenches. You were to help someone in action.

Your nausea sways beneath the trees. Stationary, the riverbank balances your fatigue, the shame of your blood. Even the best of them were gone. The best only. As he was last left. Puny. Broken.

If the ledger balances, the repetitions are less accurate, less intense, less frequent, and the time between lessons flattens. The Unnamed Soldier's entry into the ledger:

∴

I am again I am again I am transparent.

∴

My Afterdeath

Death Speaks:

∇

The trees dreamed a certain static. I dreamed I saw beauty. I dreamed you lay at the road's edge. Or was it just the grass in late sun. What toward me did you bring. This meeting of one, my conspirator. We, of no repercussion, lived once as the same body. I had always known the sun. Known winter's sandhills at midpoint. Summer is just here.

Safety is perception sometimes. Sometimes the signs are not there. Restrictions grew. We woke, iron's taste on the tongue, artillery smoke. Your lips bled mercy and thistle.

First, you used up hurt, then you gave away your neighbour. It was an open equation, a satisfaction. Your neighbour killed his neighbour. A constellation in dispersion. Do what you may. And then, again, take the gun.

I held you in the field as The Doctor packed the wound. He said it was a stitch up. No retribution came. It was simple in unity to bind myself. There was no other mark. Only this seam from another realm.

Later, in the arbour, under the eye of a tailorbird, the afternoon's small apostate, I fell into renewal.

Δ

‡

The Dead were floating cities on the river, chalk mark's glow of swollen currents. Addresses flecked the riverbank as a series of service numbers, gold fillings, and birthdates in metallic halos.

Lighthouses bade the rowers. But this was only a delusion of a shack's kerosene glint beyond the province.

You lay in the trench and listened to a shrapnel sermon; the bone-rifle click aimed at the pink hillside where captives poured through columns of banaba trees.

One fifth of the villagers vanished in the looting. A hawk streamed above the sun's basin.

Mahogany trees in the clearing signalled relief. The warriors returned drenched in the indigo aroma of spruce.

Time's diagrams and charts, unaccountable to what is writ. What was writ into the pistols, numerically etched and unetched. Fingerprint lives you would not read in The Astronomer's star-room, but who you would touch and dissolve into borealis and atoms. The lectures silenced.

The Guard was dead. And among the infantry, under orders of contempt, you sat humid and too long in the pelt of the week's rain, as others, not yet still, set the roads with landmines.

On off days you listened to birds sway unseen through arrows and fog. Mostly you were close to mercy without devotion. Yes, your accomplice, the wind, was wholly restless.

Where the kingdom's bristled pasture merged into flesh, a trick of the eye at the road to the plaza, you thought you glimpsed the school kids waving flags at the rotunda. Along the shoals, small crosses loomed beneath cottonwood.

The method was created. A genesis seeping through the swale and the ridges, the underworld rises and lowers.

And in the underworld, what once seemed madness, became cathartic. A heron in a clearing inhabits the loneliest instruction. A quiver of dusk yellows the deep eye. Shotguns cross out the fog.

You abandoned the border. In dry plains of the battlefield, now down in voiceless echoes, dust-weather mineral-covered eyes awoke, and their ribs closed under the pressure of their lungs' lacerations.

There is nothing new in hell's attractions; Magdalene drew cedar leaves around you; sandalwood smoke encircled your left palm. You received the wicked's blessing.

She snapped the stag's antler to bring the town wealth. Following that, a lark's nest of festival-tinsel, straw, and dung lodged in her larynx. She did not foresee the breech of her sixth child under the altar's spread of tektite, rice, and saffron. When there was a filter between her desires and Barachiel's guidance, she read prophecy by cracks in quail eggs.

She wrote into the ledger:

.·.

Did I tell you when I slept in the room, long years after the sky-burial, before the spell of your birth, I heard someone knocking. Shortly before moon but not before night.

.·.

How will you live now. Without ethic in death. No obligation. No personal discipline of piety. No containment.

Did I tell you of the transgressions, …bonfires' waters broken under siege. A rifleman stroked her neck as you gleamed, back-lit in oyster-shell pots of the kitchen.

By ocean's keel she stepped into membership—the stingray's velveteen skin, the foreshore's black sandbar. Hands raised, salt-blind, she swam the last meter without you.

As in the 10th century, married to the consequence of the forty suns, *I was a poison self*, a misdemeanour of flies beneath your scalp, phlox, and phlegm; glass pine needles bound you to her reflection.

‡

In precision the battalions returned from battle. Onyx camouflage slid inside fidelity's map. The borders shifted.

Magdalene caused you grief. You hear her. But if you go now, if you go in clumsy guidance, you're captive to heat's thrice signal: the sea's granite edge, the riverbank's red moss, hawthorn saplings beneath which she stood the line.

Even by accident she knew her lover's face.

It was an exchange, and she took it. She bloodlet the wounds and gathered tinctures among herons and asphodels.

‡

She inhaled the sun in a partial breath, matching the rhythm of his broken pulse. The moon's citation emerged upon the mountain. She plants a medal to his coat in pre-burial. For years you dreamed a winter sun, dreamed this accident under the grey eclipse, this night, the embalmed sky. She never said a word. You were without merit in the meritorious dark. Not safe, she watched him—her gaze was love's first offence. The French blue walls, his yes, a lichen carpet beneath the archway.

The clamp closed between contractions followed by a raw incision. Scissoring a nerve, sutures, a half stitch, a basket weave, bobbin lace as Buck's Point and closed pin kissed the last knife.

Nothing descends over the shimmering, no light blinks beyond the ridge. She didn't know how he kept shelter in hoarfrost, no demand came. No goodness wandered from the hallowed slopes where he lay. A soldier without superstition, one leaderless outcast.

In that state, semi-waking into sleep yet failing, she asked you. You sat on a lime-green stool against long planes of glass, a lake behind.

‡

In the years of the recurrent dream, you lay on the ocean floor.

You came from a small city, formally a seaport. She woke rowing through thistles, weeds, rubbish, and swamps amid your language.

You memorized rows of seagrass, a shallow whip in the mirror—low and far behind her reflection. Of the sea sound she leans toward water's flamed reflection. Motes, her lover's ash, double in a in shallow grove behind her, a buried room in which the doors prop open.

Once trauma's asphyxiation releases to ether, colour and texture dissolve and irrational thoughts are a privilege. She knows he is at is the end of the system of music.

You tried to drown the memory.

‡

The Detachment Commander was discharged before she could report the assault. Prior placements, postings, deployments, prior procedures, the faces of the men in the unit surged beneath the surface of her sleep in nightless turnings. A timeline's spasm held sway in her lower spine.

You were in the protection party for the senior delegates. With no contact, we left the command post, and drove the vehicles all afternoon through alternative routes. Spotters watched the convoy as we crossed inland detours where the farm boys' dark tongues spat before the sediment we passed. Our body-armour and helmets fogged, only a dozen bullets returned our traces.

Magdalene recorded:

∴

> *As if already the mob approached us, I drew my pistol then turned to see you with blood all over your face, your chest, the concrete blooming an oil slick beneath you. I held your mouth to my mouth, blood filling my throat. Your lungs heaved a black brine. Blood in your mouth into my mouth. Now in tunnel vision I betray your body by my wakefulness. And there it started as soon as you were gone. Our ears ringing in two theories of space. One where I touched you, not knowing you were there. One where you stood in the frame beyond me that I couldn't believe in. A channel of tinnitus prolonging our connection and separation in one unfolding as I heard only a resonance without knowing your voice. I knew no amount of gauze or press upon your sternum would hold you into the afternoon.*

∴

‡

A gurgle of flies drowned your torso when the warmth of your breath drained and the glow left your eyes. She understood. She couldn't receive whoever it was that came riding the truck's crimson crucifix. The Medic's shadow stood erect behind him as he hunched over the wreckage.

‡

As kill code, as the moment your body's other country kicks at the centre, you map the dark. It thins your body. You wanted things to be whole and perfect for a while without the question of alliance. Oil rushed your throat. She remembered the barrack where you lay; the screw reversed itself from the wall where the fingerprint smears vanished. The Distinguished Flying Cross lay on the nightstand, swath of lipstick on its obverse.

Only the smell of camphor in the small room, the texture of her hair against your cheek, a blade of light under the door streams the room into a crooked shore. A spate of storms reach the headland.

You were the first lover she told. Through sleep paralysis, you sensed violence in the button eyes of children, the baby she abandoned, The Warrant Officer's assault in the shower room, the ritual she made of hate. Whoever he came from, it happened. She hadn't heard him cry. An hourglass shrunk in a string of devotions, no more prayers, no more potency for the future. She hadn't heard him cry. She didn't cry. She didn't shout.

She measured your forearm against her hip bones. She repeated the surrender under the sun's steamed ablution. A gold spinning scent of chestnut spun the earth. She felt your fingers on her spine, the taste of your breath, the scent of vermouth.

‡

In the ledger she wrote:

∴

I remembered our knees touched as we knocked across waves.
In the splintered boat, our smallness silenced the noon tankers.
Their shadows began as blackout-tarps and paused between
our dilated eyes. Femur to femur, our steady brace.

I wanted to exit the water, for the tide to pull us apart.

∴

‡

And he, The Unnamed Soldier, replied in her mind through the page:

∴

It wasn't anyone's fault in particular. No, specifically, we could not say. As little as twice we paused. We knew. The landscape, a passed-out conscience, the palm of her hand rolled open before us. We held our suspicions, a mouth dark lexicon. Our inner charms, our personal luxuries shifted. Sublingual, familiar, she revealed in us the actions, the actions of The Dead.

∴

After the war I would no longer touch you like a stranger.

∴

THE BOURBAKI
PANORAMA

‡

You held a posting in a small room at the armoury. Not one window. Nor the sun's repetition across the terrain.

You were a supplicant on earth seeking no claim, no cause.

At the interiors at the hill camp, where prisoners lay corner to corner or in hallways with doors across and air between, it was here, among death's preparations, you lost sense of benevolence and justice for what is right. You never earned your way toward, you never showed faith, but you carried the weight. You carried retribution and you wondered about what differences exist between anyone. Like sliding doors, too late, all the office papers fell at your feet. Before there was mercy, there was ruin, before ruin: swamp wood, a delayed heartbeat. You kneeled.

Once you knew the species of a bird by a wing tip, understood the wainscoting's raindrops, runnels, and mildew patterns that signalled a humid winter. What love you learned came through the brevity of any lesson. You wondered when the year was coming back, when it was going.

Perhaps The Padre disappeared in the last evacuation. In the hours before vehicles were caught by the massacre, perhaps he was against the wall or received by the crowd, less witness as infrastructure. The episode went undefined. It seemed nothing odd happened in the night, but there, the bodies were piled. A physical process, by the guidance of maggots, three hemispheres rose into a new netherworld under skin: the newly hatched: the newly dead.

While many of the soldiers passed a cigarette between them, they couldn't talk. It did sound suspicious, her death, the virus.

There was an atmosphere of poison within this sheltered silence.

What was your name. You asked her and you asked her.

You didn't know exactly what would happen. But you knew something was about to happen. You knew each country had its own army. You knew that widebody aircraft sent medical supplies to the outlands. When you looked, directly, you knew her power. A point of stasis. She called The Dead inside. She called them to stand before her undead presence.

You were not near to her. Oddly, there was no curse to be avoided.

She came from a small city, formerly a seaport. She rowed through thistles, weeds, and swamps amid a new language. She lived solitary among the scribbled oaks. The Dead spoke through her as water spilled the lower banks at the valley's crest and flooded the blighted grass. Her voice, a host of sparrows, fled the underbrush. And later still, less distractedly and given for anyone, you replaced each star on the little sleeping horizon. The rushes sifted in the mud. A perennial lagoon, a laneway along the waterfront with an indelicate ease, she moved through the undertow.

For years you tried to address her mercenary joy. You have seen her nature, your nature. Your faults, a loneliness you've not disclosed. You've whispered it northbound to the elms, the grasses—*I tell, I tell, I tell.*

You asked her to tell you. She said—*I never saw him, though slow he came towards me— and easily. He unlocked the gate.* He was the very small silence drawn upward within the sound of the latch. Captive between captive. You, another face within his face, it was strange and true like a dirty dress dropped into a laundry basket, an ordinary act. It was as if you crawled out from a terrestrial thicket. You waited for the hunger to rise, knew, and understood your body's conjoined voice, a summer possession, heat siphoned from within her throat.

There is a lavish sickness in love.

You have never observed the spiritual. But you remember the campo, the sparse plane where the land ended.

You are going, as you said. Slowly, into your own nature. You are going mad. You see the offence of your human game. You see the little country town, the woolshed beyond wherein desire was exchanged.

‡

You agreed on the coordinates as a means of action: grasslands, a tributary that sprawled a cross-work of biomes. So after she left, you followed the line of ice along the river, crossed loose plains through the north which turned in darkness, as you turned deeper into pain, the space where your injury followed.

She was sitting and you were sitting. You were looking at your hands as a reference. Your hands, were shaking, and you didn't remember shaking. You think her name was Magdalene. You wanted to sketch her face, crosshatch the stones along the wall behind her.

The year was marked. You arrived on the street. Yet when you stood there, you saw a repetitive visual: a man on the sidewalk spitting into an oil spot as he stepped off the curb.

Magdalene's mood moved in the exacting of this man's stride—a slight impression of arrogance. It's a memory of numerous reversals that have been suffered as a form of love. Her instincts grew into duty without privilege.

That night you approached her at the makeshift house. Indigo soil settled in thick filaments throughout her hair as the lamp lowered over the table rocking the wind's switchbacks.

‡

That's one telepathic reading on the situation, and certainly, there are other projections in an excess of various directions. You knew they'd find vendors that would collect their souls after they died.

You were another face within her face. She could see you as if looking through glass fields. You slept by lakeside reeds. Your ribs, objects of resistance, a war plate.

You slept alone, and if she were to find you at night, your body lay as a knot, a singular scar in its ghost pattern.

‡

Unable to hide, your blemish. In well-doing, you died with peace.

If you wanted to be held alive, you'd wish for mediumship.

‡

The woman is obscure now. Refined and symbolic in her slightness, she is a sharp tear in the atmosphere where the idea of her body remains. She is given less. Given the cold. Given the earth's diagram. The mottled bruises around her thighs were like paled seedlings in a hexagonal pattern. The amber bees faded around her into a bronze wax, a sheen, an aura of her last fight. The gold leak of light under the door swelled between her teeth and tongue, a sugary passport, a taste you may quiet, as you quiet your envy. You thumbed a scented oil over the centre of her forehead. You absolved all connection.

You sit in her mind with objectivity. You sit in her mind, an oceanic ghost. You learn to adapt to what you must relinquish. What must you relinquish. She held out documents you could not read. Anthracite threads of her dress were the river's current, green ink smeared waters, lines grafted through currents like snakes among sand and leaf litter. You unlearn sympathy. You pin her in the woods to a small town. You seal the papers in nectar and think how you might gather her secrets. A glass cloche closes over shadow. And beneath glass, inside the shadow: a wall. Beyond the wall a walkway filled with Venus-blue insects trapped in mudstone. In another dimension there is a woman who travelled to the wasteland to keep The Dead safe from the blazing houses. The newspapers stated that she eloped from the room to look for an exit, but she entered one fire into another. She entered a room where all the doors were blocked.

You took nothing.

You've mostly been a non-being. Perhaps you have always been a non-being, streaming in the waves, conscious of the hand which might protect or release you. You were a seer and saw the balm she soothed like fuel over the blades of grass on the embankment.

You spoke so reasonably the night the barbarians came.

No, this probably isn't the truth. You challenged The Dead in your shape taking, your obtuse nature. You adhered to a deeper restlessness.

‡

Today Yesterday Hereafter

Death Speaks:

∇

How could I say I'd studied her. The O of my blood, the liquid trees now gone to winter. Birds couldn't wake me.

*

I write to give her my identity; she is in the tight edicts where light obscures my dreams. To tie yourself to The Dead is to provide truth to the abasement. A bank of reeds separates the past in lustful silence. A gentle hand pulls me through barbed wire. My same hand falls asleep now under my night pillow, where I clutch at the grass—a space where the seer's myth pressures the earth's crust. I am possessed by bereavements, as a number is assigned and tagged to my right breast. I witness a series of horses emerge—microdots in the paddock, harbingers. Beneath the north-mare's flank, ticks burrow into foal's skin, energy consecrates mediumship's awakening. The foal was dead, but when I flip it, the foal is vapor. To look I can't see. So I enter.

I am not so originally silent but am angled and broken as I lean against the midnight house and watch her rest.

The night I left is not the beginning of desire's autopsy.

The body is an energy field unwonted. The landscape is just too easy, and I am reluctant to cross. Being human requires living in terror.

I've kissed the lonesomeness in your body on being love in your body and love on the body.

I plied open your mouth each time. I was thorough. I adjusted the barricade. Possession is spiritual. My own sense of prophecy was received—a nameless manifestation of tenderness.

It took days before my last purpose. Before I could walk there into that space of my death. And finally, your mouth would open like you knew the word.

I walked through the discourse. I followed the voice committed to the aspen, the spike-moss, the granary. Still the sand hills were high in Oxbow and they divided into an expanse of alder trees upward behind the pharmacy.

Among the alder trees, in simple pieces, I reconstruct my sleep. I reconstruct with all my tools, a new occupation. I inhabit you. I follow you up the banks and we search the sides of shadbush for a trail. Nothing left of the birches, simply a snow broken over the river where the horses came. The horses climb now out of the rivers and onto the lanes of plane trees. They are nothing like we remembered. Nor those they carried. They were no credit to the river, to the things done, to what they emptied themselves of. Held there. Oblivious, whole, and dull off stockyard shadows.

Wood vetch grows upon banks, near the sides of hedges. O there is nothing to conceal over this almost naked, over this almost skin, this once considered vast. It is almost without pleasure.

Δ

‡

You believe your loved ones requested certain fields. You believed certain transmissions within fields equated to your faith.

There is a freedom in this circumstance, the arrival to this outpost where you may engage sensations apart from consciousness. Perhaps you'll never step away from your homeland. Perhaps you'll deliver your desire as a new interest in love.

You've gone into the quiet grass and left her with your back turned to the promontory. The sea's skin stiffens, and waves like pearled lips crack in the heat's madness. Will you ever feel strange by the way The Dead show themselves to you?

They were no credit to the river, to the things done, to what they emptied themselves of. Held there. Oblivious. And bright off stockyard shadows.

It grows upon banks, near the sides of hedges. O there is nothing to conceal over this almost naked, over this almost skin, this once considered vast. It is almost without pleasure.

Yet they and this were your beloved. They were bought of loose maps, stones, trespass of snowshoe.

You are like they. And now they are one, beyond anything now else.

You try to interweave the code of your body's transmissions through time and space. Not to demarcate a series of events but devise the cellular impact of a new lexicon; perhaps, a foetal barnacle, a growth expanding from the old one that you still recognize.

You will not close your heart to language. It is the transmission which connects you to symbol. Phrase by phrase to grandmothers and fathers so far past.

You spoke so reasonably the night the barbarians came.

‡

Bees buckled the canvas sun, a paradigm for heat's mutation over the lawn where the dandelion's white roots and burnt grass tangled into an earthen tarp. No movement. No one but you. So you disappeared beneath it. She stared at your throat where camouflage married your jawline, that landscape's ridge entering your voice where healing splits from humiliation. She felt your pride. A marginalia of blood stains and oil spots framed the ledger's parched pages.

∴

Is it you there I dread? The voices crowd the room. Is everyone in the room leaving? I suppose I would like to die. When eyes will allow it. I imagine it's like a solitude that doesn't happen. But I'm not expectant. Not restless. I have use of the voices still, of my own voice. It happens. It happens.

∴

‡

What the dreamer dreams through mourning is masked as owl, as in a false owl, tar and feather pressed spine, faded eyes pointing east, an unsafe wisdom of clay, paper, woodchip. Speech was forward blown between us and discarded, as was history, simple as chance cigarette-ash fallen after sex passes. *We did not die in our dying,* she said.

But in truth, as it is known, we did. Your small armaments, my ritual persuasions, amulets held you unweary. They said that you must lie down, allow very little movement, no more pacing the veranda; but just past your view of the lane you could see her near the grove. She lay among the famine swept passages of oak leaves layered in spring decay.

Your anatomy thins into Kodachrome. You hide in a plastic box, a luminescent cue, a white vibration on the edge of the film. Through pinhole you were an upside down oceanview, a pollen breeze, a film that stilled the water's backdraft and, through glass, appeared pearly.

It seems natural now. In one eyepiece you are there, on the other side, a paper crane. And to the furthest plane you moved so quickly.

You latched a velvet rope around the burning snapshots of the cathedral, followed her, knew you could work further with your mind. You sat near the small girl in the casket, and recited five words from the canticle: 'let me hear your voice…'

You kneel beside her slight body, into her sleep's end, and in guilt's attribution weave violets in her black braids before covering her to the earth. Dried chrysanthemums garland her throat. Bronze coins seal her eyelids.

In musk, in milkwood decay, in hours named as failure, in all attrition…

The going on next happens, a script at the desk with quill, your cadence of paperwork fills the senses. From the room of the immortals, you make your note. Possible is the trauma. You tell her where to stop. What evil happens.

You tell her to document another of your dreams:

∴

…and it featured your anteroom (nothing like this room I am in now with its books, stuffed pillows, taxidermy bittern) surrounded in walls of drawers overflowing with writings, little statues and badges, a basket of all the missing shoes (just one of a pair) plunked under a cot upon which you sat cross-legged. A lady's small haven, a space to calculate numbers and study hieroglyphs…

∴

‡

The Sun Republic: Hereafter, Magdalene

Death Speaks:

∇

Under the bell wheel, the moon of the shortest day fell under the moon that signalled the furthest sun. I couldn't imagine what I wanted, but never I understood why. The work continued, under execution of a certain pointlessness in the annunciation of winter, as the conflicts of the battalion drew toward me. My currencies for love remained shallow. It was somewhat like his kiss returning. A rush of water recedes, the ocean floor presses salt through my breath and in heat, suspended along the back channels—over wetlands, over smokehouses, over old smudge pits—I pass through the chalk-smeared home where my lover vanished.

In a stream, in a line of sight, as in the first line of my vision, I fingered a loop and a cross.

L⊃⫠Ϲ

And I stood before myself as a dreaming woman.

I too lived as, and without, an enemy. But that was long before.

Not much troubled me once the planets dropped, shadowy and scissored between the trees. Silence was swallowed behind the boulders, and the hill beyond them shifted. I'd done with my life what I could to help others. I faced the advancement. Though I'd been ordered to step down. I didn't recognize the judgment. The little town and distant smoke rings disappeared in the atmosphere of defeat. It was quite dark. Into dark's heavy rest I went. Cedar trees splintered the canyon. Trains advanced in a thousand bolts. I etched tracks into feldspar and The Dead petroglyphs denoted new insects, new signals of the colonist's settlement.

We were always the first in battle.

This might have been my first return, but it wasn't.

I was born this, not known in song. I was born without a ledger, yet the ledger recorded the dialect—and I spoke from omen's word, I spoke from the soft mouths of the lost.

§

In another century I lived in the abbey at the mid-shore where my body-wheel broke clay, broke wheel, opened and broke again, star-spike, wood spine.

Yes, in the other century, I lived on the outer province. I lived in the orchard before it was cleared for farms. I died without ruin. I died understanding the obscure drawings as an unspoken code. I died continuously. Under the poplar's bald branches, at knifepoint, The Dead's language pressed beneath my chin.

There was no inhabited world, but I went under. The inhabited world fell away. Just as it always had.

I would leave life just as if I left the view from the window.

My conscience didn't belong below bright birch roots, nor above in spring's papery crescent-shaped buds. I had to understand who I was within the ease of this new amber landscape. It is a time of haunting of time. Under the starched sky, a burnt sail lifted me. In the sun republic, I didn't recognise the burial celebrations or The Farrier walking home after death, walking home to see his dead brother. Under what recurrence, born to this world, but not this life, could I touch the boundary of the dark, the sun governing each impression, each bird's pulse. Mistaken ghost, I arrive—in trenches, as solar birdsong, I creep into the night like a spill of milk over the lake.

If I paid attention to the light's vessel, to wingbeat, my hand would press directly over the water and brush the inquiry of distance, the sea ascending to cloud, my eye, visible through periscope, the space in which sleep is made hollow. I would be filled with the glance of your belonging.

I must preserve the story. I cannot know their age, or where they are from, or the crest over which they may be gazing.

Winter cut its threads behind me, a trail of coattails and possum furs; November's spear grass shredded the ravine.

Rusted marigolds bloomed as the survivor's fresh artillery. I would remember this as winter hunted. Unaccountable, I embodied the meadow's parallel, twilight's vernacular, the crisscross gnash of horse whip.

So far in love, I followed you down from the lane. I fell into the patterns, the weathers. In order to hear you. It was the kind of winter one might read in strangeness. Snow's patterns spread over the lake as an odd subscript for loneliness. I read the geese's formation. I'd disappointed you. I lived in the open with the invaders. I told you what I was seeking from my country and from what country I sought my mind.

There was nowhere I had to live, so I opened the door to the other lives we carried. A labour began. A spiritual killing crawled up from the sea's edge.

We were always the last in battle.

§

The Dead told me to take off my war paint. I saw not a single soldier, not another dead brother, not a single ghost in the border. I came through the rewards, and the rewards came through the course of it. The rewards came as a girdle of heron stretched over the grasslands. The void held no specificity.

I never conjured your loss—but they say my tongue spelled it. I lived only in the wood-season and met you in visions. I woke in you a waking sleep, a sensitivity within the realm of the battle. I never distrusted your safety, because I wasn't weak among our tyrants, but somehow, I'd led the attack. I blamed the tenderness of your stride, your lame descent as they advanced. I refused to forgive, dearest, your invisible boundary, the ruptured arrow.

On our feast day a thousand rifles paused. The men's necks broke in sweat as they lay down their weapons. I saw them cross the ridge before they crossed the ridge. The earth became ceiling as the sky bottomed out into a million winds. Particles mingled between us and the enemy. I would walk west, across the snow basin just as I've always done to collect stones, firewood, and buckets of sap. Without protection, my father's shadow arrived at the river. Spokes of the river centralized. At this small altar of pines, his birch-streaked phrases named the sequence of his days, and he told me a secret as if from an old seer. I'd fight a sergeant. In killing him, his chest would crack like pottery, chrysanthemums would splay over a lagoon. His battalion would attack, would kill my whole family.

The Seer's notes are recorded in the ledger:

∴

In the past your indecision created deaths for others. You lost your temper and shot an arrow in the sergeant's shoulder, creating a massive attack which killed your tribe. But you lived. You became very old.

∴

I'll carry this abandonment on into the next life. I'd leave through the mountain's centre, a thin edge of boulders where I could hide in a cave near the gulch.

Remorse only came when I left the elders. Loyal in grief. They washed his blood from my hair, my feet, my arms. They spoke to me in gesture. I remember this now. A time I was loved just after a time in which I hated.

The minute they emptied my wound I knew how to undress the world's external habits. I held dignity in my desires. Not because I am human, but for the fact I believed in language, it is logic's singular energy.

§

Sometimes the dead settlers followed me home. They longed to buy me flowers of their innocence. The innocent dead in innocent deaths. They are curious men whom most can't see. I am made useless by their devotions. I am made endless. I couldn't see the seekers, the patriotic addicts hidden by sun's profile. I was like a scythe meant to flatten the grasses over the thick fields of tripwire. But I could never show them the way back.

In the meadow chamber, the solitary ones approached. In my mind, I touched the air of their arrival. Waves of green stalks aligned into a single spine along the windowpane. I finger the salt marsh as it flutters in a watermark on the glass.

A quick flit of leaves lowered the flats. Her temples burned. I stood for an hour, my hand pressed to the glass, revibrating with the heat of flies as if a portal would open, or I'd be lifted from the spot on the clapboard floor.

There is a staking of houses in the revenant's paddock; conjoined by his fence, I, a neighbour, live in a barn—stump beneath stump—where rain taps upon and upon. My garden is a silo's wood planks among wild potatoes. Undoubtedly, I will be buried here. Each night the holy grass opens a sphere where I lay. In my dreams, a talc sediment dissolves over the round; you visited me, came into my body, and I carried you as a three-day sludge in my belly. My likeness, my captor. Within the limit of one, a genesis.

At this foreshore of the sun there is a town I frequent. Walking there I feel the winter boats heave beneath my throat. My breath eases like blades of wheat flooded by the water's sheen. Snow fills my lungs.

I sat in the local pub all winter. Not earthbound but enfolded by hewn coral brick walls. Under my booze belt, I stare at a portrait of a woman perched above the corner table. When I look at her, she introduces me to myself. Her eyes are the star's doorway he and each of The Dead entered, the dissolving lagoon, the seven origins of the last four streets he lived.

Darling, he's gone, she says.

The man at the table behind me eavesdrops; my voice allows his silence. Grief's careful telling of love's name is a clumsy dialogue. Signals were arriving.

They said it was impossible, but when the nurse described the amputee from the war hospital, I knew it was you.

The Dead took me through several lives to arrive at the hospital tent. I found the dressing station and the nurse who attended to his typhoid. *We couldn't bury him,* she said. He lay undressed. *I told him to relax. He knew you were coming, but I didn't think he'd make it,* she said.

Dead he is now. And I, too, flung into the frozen stars. I've eaten the creosote. The poison of the surface stream, the fourth reality of time: a flat surface, dusk in the mouth, the soiled sheets, straw mattress, his body nothing but weeds. Reality, a flat surface. It would be easy to say that I am dead. But I am not restive.

In my way above the map, I am grieved.

Each morning, more alleyways bombed, more predilection considered as meaning.

One might say it was possible, but from my experience it wasn't.

You never appeared in the valley.

Still radiant, the sound of wind, an aria in the chamber grass, the sea's washup, where driftwood crosses pale the shoreline. I lie open into the sound. Bells swarm the thicket—dusk breaks the river wide; a dozen bees, the sea hawk's trill, daylilies burnishing the coast. The madman lived on absence, a winter boat mooring beneath his throat, a single blade of wheat: the water's sheen. Snow haemorrhages the lungs—the first white heavies a pigeon's wing.

§

Today and yesterday, my afterdeath, I eased into the small boat. I couldn't abstain the waters, the channel beneath the bridge beneath the other bridge, the wild duck pond into which all the ships moor. And as I remembered my death and I remembered my birth, I forgot the sacrament, the pledge, the waves pillage as water softens stone.

We are another kind of ending. She and I.

I must consider the salvation worthy stars, the ones which dip above the horse trough, minutes after noon, when word by word the earth's activation is neutral. I must examine myself.

There is a permeable reality where time and distance acquire certain progressions. I might examine my regrets.

She was not pitying. But unsettled. Some goddess I wanted to claim.

What were we to make of our injuries. The water is always sweet in the furthest world. Warriors, under heavy artillery, killed or wounded from the inside, though only small entry holes were visible on their skulls.

The cries slide up through the trenches, a powder hangs above the clay mounds and wires, layers of lace, a bride's tulle, floats serene over the black earth. Not the enemy now, as a low kindling pressed beneath fog, but the train of her gown drags us forward. Over the splayed grass, a sovereign silk, our location is expressed in waves beneath her skin, we felt the needling beneath the searchlight's last crossing in spring.

I will never be alone now that I've known her.

We looked up into the ether, hand in hand. Beside me she lay in protection. Alive, filled with traces of home. We were made bare. No mechanism kept us safe now. We listened to the estuaries' slow, skeletal practice, small trickles, an ebb. Reinforcement troops swept the parameters. While once, out to sea, we'd been filled by a perfect victory.

Δ

‡

You were captured, my captor, and all you wanted drew into a bend at her throat as she eased back, pushed back, against the grass and the shade brushed between her lips.

Your skin, to her skin, your alpha and omega, as her wound grew nearer, grew in you, blistered into a perfect crush against your rib.

What you began in the imagination was without memory. It is the first magic. It's a sun. You each accentuate: your eyes as black coins, two pupils dilate, a betweenness. In all this spectacle could she see you? Could she say the dark went smiling as you emerged through it, or say more pointedly, that your dark smile emerged as you moved through her into the night-kill, as killer. As love.

As if, in the bounds of a safe agency, as if aiding an enemy, alone, under a cool possession, this secret betrayal bound you. She could see you. In her eyes you'd already passed through her.

∴

> *Under the pine, his eyes over and in. My assassin, my love. My perfection. A perfection in the mouth of the mouth of whose name. Mine, the first life I knew, and the last.*

∴

‡

Death Speaks:

∇

The adventure of my breath met them in the quiet, as if on a wild acreage, I sent them my protections, consecrated visions, a safe afterdeath. Mother, I am here in the boat and the bridge and the bells. I am the dream. I am the ringing. In the dream of common sobriety, I am impossible with erosion, derision. The surge in my body is my body.

I am a vagabond, weak and relentless. It was the understanding you held for me. The slim stretch of sea, a seam the horizon stitched. Accept this one disclosure, corporeal, the rendering of my need, as your need. May you accept one, as you can accept me, accept my death. My appointed horizon is satisfied by this view.

O line of sawdust, line of gravel, line of asphalt, line of milk.

We placed ourselves in the field. Our top cover gone, this now hit us, we relinquished. Trust fractured.

When I could see you, I could see your death.

I didn't know how to do it. How to tell you that from my perspective of the accident, our unfortunate actions, neither malice, nor omission, no dilution, no evidence, only regret. Orphan of clamour, silence residual in your tongue, this waking. Among the almost. Among the vanished. The origin of speech binds history. It was easy to use, you were eased.

I carried, so it was, the only movement, a personal blackout among the blacked-out stars, a bloodied bloodshed between blows. Peace never arrived. No holy campaign, no pilgrimage.

I recalled the flames rising through the startled edge of the wind.

A tympanic pause broke the glade open. Your breath stuttered; you were an absence under skin. Your body's source sunk. A veil of wasps shored above us. Midnight dropped below us as loam, the wagtails and longclaws stole the air.

Under a breeze, a thousand blossoms, the names of the horses fell away.

Those who came running came into living.

The mare's strange quiescence just as she touches the river. Wandering bees stretch into a hidden spot above her forehead. They circle into the shape of a cat's ear, sugar scented, stray.

An industry of balance held each whisker, just at the right speed. Wax-papery leaves, white exhalation, snow blowing down unto my well-formed path.

I learned. I made praise of learning. The stations of love are a brightness, a singing.

The line moved forward.

In the year of that year, the year of crusades which scored twelve centuries, I sought home. Home, the terms of my blindness, a blackout where the sun crossed the road, and gathered red at the curve. *Why did you dwell into what you dwelled*, I said. Sometimes. I carried my kindling into the spark into the one dark fire beyond the dark under the circumstance of my distance.

You accepted, in late September, my repatriation. In retribution, restless with the longing seen by the other body, seen by the shadow which infused my light, you accepted my dangers, my inhibitions, by inhabitations.

The year finished.

§

I cared for the horses that stood at the side of the road. Dash marks along the pastoral, they held no story.

You said sometimes they die and sometimes you have a hand at cutting the small animals out of those who are meant for a bullet.

Your voice was right when you said it. Still with logic.

I had given them apples and droppings of hay gathered outside the shelter where I stayed each night.

There is a fragrance of tea and a snowflake on the roan's brow. There is a flickering and a light through a vast canopy of cloud, a luminous door through which my voice drowns.

I would stand by them in the rain if needed. I am determined. But it never rains here. I had a body and no idea how long it would last. I couldn't say I loved them. But they were my last brothers in the human world. We lived in a secret. Some gifts are unwanted. The mare, heavy with foal, wades in exile as the laws of traffic cede. The metallic sound, a heron's wing, beams across the sown field.

§

Perhaps this is compassion. It is happily without need. It makes no associations. To what I've adjusted, you listen. You listen and we cross the bridge, the atmosphere between the whole of our body creates a strange ease. The spring valley, a crossroad where a house shrinks on the horizon.

Yes, I fed the horses, but was it *"I"* in the story. Was it *"you"* in the story. I don't remember. But I remember the pasture. I remember standing among them. And when I held out my hand they came to feed. They fed from the grain to feed me.

I have learned carefully to love and to fight among the traitors. I am careful now.

Somewhere the body unloads itself of time. But that's just perception. The horses I groom, visible in the field to a passer-by, are said to be alive. They are said to be alive, but honestly, I couldn't see them.

There is place in the self beyond sleep. Yes, there is a sleep in which there will be an hour, a ridgeline. You'll walk upward into the bronzed rocks. There is a room there. And a horizon which you will not believe. Perhaps the room is a space for love. And what love's room became in us is a trance under a passing wheel—the awkward sun, a sun possessed—a landscape's wet spark—useless words you begin to forget or nevertheless remember as I track your brief descent.

I didn't know you could be summoned from the lonely ground among the lumen and the earth and the wind through pin-oaks.

Your people in this place had been shoved into each margin. And our progress of lifting each injustice was like a sipping of air, as the air drowns our lungs. Every molecule around us moved within us.

§

You start. You are filled in silence. Death quietly reaches one way. One way I fought the other. I knew you would tell me to pick one. A she, or a her, an I or a you. But consciousness is multi-fold. I refuse.

Δ

‡

The leaves spill over her brow.

You are receiving, as you did, a certain shadow of passion.
Were you a human.

Perhaps you are the horse; perhaps you are misguided.

O the horse, the one misguided and marked for the effort, the
one to store and bury The Dead. War bells ring at noontime.
You would be foreign to the one account—

The sleeper's hand is curled. A dry night has come.

‡

Death Speaks:

▽

Anchored to the grass, in the split dark between doors, I give myself over plainly to myth. The understory gives plainly, word by word, to the earth's mantle. Through one door, your messages flooded the room. Through the other, in periphery, I saw willowy figures dart. They lived as apparitions in the night's various levels. They waited for love. They lived, hallucinogenic: triangles and fractal neon patterns, peonies Agrippa, red or pale tamarisk, scent of glasswort and smoke-rings, they floated moonlit up the wall. Somewhere in all of this, a horizon exists, a farm on the other side of the small woods. Among the mayapple, chokecherry bushes brush against your wrist, a first kiss, but not the first body.

I think of you in the earth, think of you beneath my fingers, plum-shaded loam.

And the rocks turned black and threw up shadows and the shadows on the rocks were like birds as they lifted themselves and flew, only they did not fly. They hung still.

And the stars wrecked me.

Δ

‡

Dreaming the Barbarians…

You did not know you were dead, that you were unguarded,
inconstant

>   you were offered a glass of water, thirst lost in your
>   hand,

there were no others, no sentries,

>   no constellation in the crack of the door,   if you
>   were one

without consequence, where would you turn,

>   you were willing, you were refused, you were not
>   seeking but saw,

there was no way to make infinite,

>   no means by which, not to accept

the gatekeeper pressed your face to the wall, holding your
wrist, stealing your wallet—

the hazard of your city, the lesser hallway open, no crawl
space, you were too tall,

the animal was eaten and given back, by one affection, by
briar patch, by word

this was compassion, in the meantime forsythia blanche,

a gloss off ochre wool catches your sleeve, you were found
mere, your imprint of almost witness, you were marred, you
were married, and the hardest part, to get there, to make end,
O compatriot, O chawbacon,

you were the bell-wheel, combat-footage, the breath I began,
my surrender in brine

how do I touch what I love, a beggar, a waif in the rye, some
plain-clothed field assassin—

    there was catharsis, no undertaking,

in front of the cobblestone row houses, the knife-hand to the
chest in the fight,

    you were target point, perhaps, there was no other
instinct to fail between the living, no coercion between
polemics, there was no accident between the deserters, they
were unbeauty, they were seekers, and gunners, sent in body
armour and helmet, they were panic in the wake, for the
weapon, the gun mount

    the guillotine, the cavalry,   were you last in
    agreement,

           were you molecule by molecule, arrival
    subdued by light, were you landscape against the
    assembled horses, netted, nondirective

you were held to the bridge above bush-marsh, above salt
paddock,

funerary crimson undone upon your lips,

                Ophiuchus burst the sea wall,

You were in the capture, the mercy, your home had no
name, time readied you, you said there was "no separate,"
threadbare was your red mourning jacket, magnolias spilled
the sun-caldron inside the sun, and the sun

    inside your chest was a portal—your offering,

you came closer—held your father's hand, you knew

your surrender went untold by witnesses and drew a
benevolent sketch,

when you were among the tribe, when you were stripped of
spectres, who came through the others, who came to speak to
me in vesper,

in the end you asked where your glasses with the bent frames
went, the chirp of the walls were the minute, it was the un-
going, what was alone, grevillea's dappled needling,

all that you needed in the acreage,

        you gave way, sprays of rockweed, milksap

Maureen Alsop is a psychologist and author of seven collections of poetry including *Arbor Vitae*; *Tender to Empress* (visual poetry); *Pyre*; *Later, Knives & Trees*; *Mirror Inside Coffin*; *Mantic*; *Apparition Wre*n (also a Spanish Edition, Reyezuelo Aparición, translated by Mario Domínguez Parra); and several chapbooks.

PUBLISHED BY ERRATUM REPRINTS

The Scourge of Villanie
John Marston

Civilisation Its Cause and Cure
Edward Carpenter